Hangover of Fun

Agniwesh Garg

Vitasta

Vitasta Publishing Pvt. Ltd.
New Delhi

Published by
Vitasta Publishing Pvt. Ltd.
2/15, Ansari Road, Daryaganj,
New Delhi - 110 002

ISBN 978-93-80828-36-7

Cover Design by Manoj Kumar
Layout by Vitasta Publishing Pvt. Ltd.
Printed by Vits Press, New Delhi

Dedicated to

My beloved family members;
Asia Pacific Institute of
Information Technology, my alma mater;
E.coli (a super special appearance);
and
to the great recession

Author's Note

To become a writer, what can be the best platform to type down experiences other than engineering life?

To start with, this can be the perfect idea. But, at the same time as an author, sometimes it becomes so difficult to write down the realities of life. And finally, during this whole process I have learned to live with all that happened during those four beautiful years.

This story all begins with the friendship with one of my good friends, Softy and then continues ahead with Teddy. As the story progresses, the story has got different characters with the differ ent roles to perform and they are all my good friends. Overall, this whole story was a dream project for me during the last semester of my engineering and is of course a try to support one of my good friends Mini as a character in the story.

In simple lines, the story is all about friendship, unnecessary brawls among the friends and its enhanced consequences which doesn't figure out anything, rather happens and makes life engaged and hence beautiful.

To be exact; the story ahead which you'll read has got everything in it about the engineering college life. While reading the story you can have glimpses of your life in it, could be more even. As a reader or a student, whenever you want to recall those sweet memories from your college life, this ensures for you to do that.

Dear readers, the big question------- is there any existence for the "love forever" concept in the world?

I request you all, just fix up your index finger and the thumb parallel, and exactly with same quantum of life experiences, I have tried to type down this story. Life, sometimes comes up with some unexpected turns for which we never plan for and hence, if that unexpected turn is bitter, we cry for that or try to avoid that and if that unexpected turn is sweet, we carry that sweetness for the whole of our life and make our life beautiful.

Love!! Is the best thing to happen in life. Hadn't there been a fight between Peter and Teddy, the "love story" part of the story couldn't have been written. Actually, with the justification of carrying a research work was never the best idea for me to fall in love with a girl from my first neighboring country. But, naturally I allowed myself to fall in love with that girl, without knowing the absolute end for the same. And she was definitely like an angel from somewhere in paradise and blessed me forever for my life...

Contents

A little intro...

Hello everyone. I hope you will enjoy the *Hangover of Fun*. This is the first time I am writing without having any idea about writing. I am a "non-technical software engineer" and my friends call me "Golu" with love, hate, affection and care.

Below is a short testimonial written by one of my good friends on the social networking site Orkut, which I feel describes me best:

"Now here, I'm attempting one of the most dangerous tasks in my life, i.e., describing a versatile and amazing person like him within the limitation of just 1,024 characters....

"To begin with he is an infinite source of energy.... Something like a nuclear reactor or volcano doesn't know but he is....

"Also his imagination... I guess Pablo Picasso would have rented few ideas from him.

"As a human being I guess very few people know him.... he keeps so much within himself but when he lashes out you are left with no option but to run for cover. One just cannot confront him.... The bottom line is you just can't win with him.

"I thank God that I have him as my friend. He is a precious gift to me from college and I think all his other friends think the same about him; lastly I would like to say thank you Golu for being my friend..."

***

As a beginner...

"Ok Maa, see you later! Bye Papa! Please take lots of care!!" These were the words with which I left for one of the most historic places in India: Panipat. An ancient, beautiful city where three great battles had already been fought in the past. This was all that I knew about it anyways....

During the long journey, I was giving some serious thought to my grade points, ambition and life; the upcoming four years seeming nothing short of a fourth war. I was filled with nervous excitement.

A very pleasant and rather memorable morning brought me to the city that was to become my second home. It brought with it the occasion of moving into one of the most promising engineering colleges in India and a dream of starting my own 'engineer' dynasty.

The city, the college and I had at least one thing in common–we matured at the same pace. City in its infrastructure, me and my college in confidence. I reached the campus at around ten, happy to see that the hundreds of other newcomers there would soon no longer be strangers to me.

Everyone was keen to make a good start and find the perfect college mate, and most seemed cautious around their gender counterparts. I got my lucky breakthrough during the meeting with the administrative officer, where I ran into Softy. Softy looked like any of those toned-up guys in health drink advertisements, but with a distinctively delicate look. So I named him "Softy." There were two other guys who I befriended, though they were not as good as Softy.

First day was all about shifting luggage, understanding each other and adjusting to the new environment. The sumptuous dinner, gossip and campus roaming was the icing on the cake.

I went to bed early, loyal to my father's strictly-imposed theory – *early to bed and early to rise* with pretty thoughts of freedom and the beginning of a new life.

***

Bunking lectures

Our official introduction into the college happened on the following day, starting off with a brief introduction and welcome speech from the director and the dean of the college. However, the motivational element in it ended when the rules of absenteeism were stated; we were just allowed twelve leaves in a semester! They seemed to be inculcating professionalism in us from day one.

We moved to our lecture rooms immediately after that, waiting for our respective mentors. This time I spent observing the interesting things happening all around, including the fact that the girl to boy ratio was 3:37! This rather lamentable development was also being noticed by another guy to whom I introduced myself, shaking hands.

He began, "Hi, I am 'Teddy' from…."

"It's ok," I interrupted, "it's fine with me with your name only. It doesn't matter from where you belong." As it was, I was there with him only to offer my sympathies about the ratio of the students.

"We will manage...," I whispered, half to myself,

nodding at the girls.

"Manage…?," he spluttered, "How can we compromise dear? ...Oh my goodness, you seem to be a gay."

"No way dude!" I retorted, feeling trashed. "Never! I am not like that, you got me wrong…," I managed to say, my lips stretched with the effort of keeping myself under control. "I am a fun-loving kind of person just like you. Only thing is, I can't go after a girl wasting my time and putting myself in trouble. I have never opened up my heart to a girl. That is all so unexciting for me. Life is fine without a girl and is going on quite efficiently."

The words came pouring out of my mouth, as it was the first chance I had had to explain my 'Female Theory'.

He said slowly, "It's ok man, I think I like you, except for that girlfriend theory. Definitely we have similarities. We can be friends. Let's be friends…"

"Friends forever..." I replied and shook hands with my first apparent friend in college.

"So, want to attend this boring lecture of Information Systems…?," I asked him with a grimace, hoping he'd have similar thoughts about it like me.

"Suck and run," he shot back; a phrase that was soon to become an indelible part of our college lingo.

"We need to move out of here," Teddy continued, nodding towards the door.

"So let's have some fun," I said in agreement, and we moved to the cafeteria for tea.

It was around 5:30 in the evening when some other students from our class entered the cafeteria. They all were whispering about the subject, the assignments, and most darkly about the personality of the lecturer. I asked a guy, who later on was named as "Khauf."

"Hey what's up dude? What happened? How was the lecture?"

The way poor Khauf explained the situation it seemed like the earth had been shifted to a place where there was a scarcity of oxygen. He actually looked out of breath too.

He explained uncomfortably–"Look guys, we have to complete two hardcore-sucking individual assignments, one group work and one external paper for this module alone and we have another five more modules waiting after that. Not to mention surprise tests, quizzes and ground rules, and–"

"Stop!" Teddy interrupted, cutting short the dreadful narration thankfully. "Your time is over now and you better get over it. Stop nailing my ears, otherwise just suck and run.

While enjoying my fourth tea with the snacks and wonderful background music on the television, I observed that Khauf had just changed into a tiny particle by the thunderbolt reply of Teddy. I had to intervene, to console Khauf who looked horrified.

"Friend, everything will be alright. Just have patience and be confident. Just chill, there is nothing to worry," I said softly, patting his arm.

"And what the hell are those ground rules? Are they part of this bloody module?," I asked him curiously, trying to make him feel comfortable in the conversation though requesting him to keep his answers short and simple this time around.

"No friend, ground rules are not the part of this module. But, they are the part of mind-set of the lecturer."

It includes basic rules to be followed by the students during the lectures. The most frustrating one is that the lecturer himself can pick any-one of us and ask questions. And there are many more nasty ones.

"Would you like to listen?"

"Tell him we are not bothered at all of those rules, we are the high fliers," I replied loftily, "I mean, we will face the situation whatever it be. Why to bother or panic now?"

"So you guys don't bother about all that I said?. How come you can be so careless becoming these so called high fliers?" Khauf replied looking at both of us with a stunned face.

"Yes, by bothering you can't make your life any easier," I replied coolly, and Teddy nodded approvingly.

Looking at our smiling faces, Khauf said hollowly, "I don't think I can survive here. Ohh God! Where am I trapped?"

***

My first encounter

It was getting dark and we were moving to our rooms after attending some consecutive lectures. I was with Softy and other room-mates. A very healthy discussion was going on between us on the day's outcome. I wasn't involved in it, but was learning a lot by just listening to the others.

They were having a clash of opinion on the issue of Mr Narang being so tough with the students.

"He has such a rude attitude. If you ask me, it's nothing more than showbiz," Softy said, shaking his head.

"Mark my words. One day we'll end up having a heated argument with him." Others were nodding their heads in agreement, and the leadership potential in my delicate friend became visible to me. But I still felt they were making a hell out of nothing.

And then one of my room-mates asked me, "Why you are not speaking at all?"

In all, honestly, I had nothing to share with them. I said, "Look it's better to take a good sleep than get involved in a great discussion. You guys carry on with your words.

I have nothing to offer for now."

Softy interjected snidely, "Yes, you have lots to offer for those stupid fellows in the cafeteria. But, it's ok."

I couldn't understand the emotional feelings expressed by Softy and rather went out for a chilled beer at a nearby shop as it was too hot and humid, thinking how could somebody lay claim to me. It was total rubbish.

When I came back to my room, two of them were busy with their pet girlfriends on the phone. I really welcomed the new situation and relaxed a lot. I found peace of mind. I opened my book and continued studying programming concepts for an hour along with my favourite songs but finally…*to hell with those concepts*. I went to bed saying good night to my three room-mates and at last the day concluded on a happy note thanks to the super cool beer. I thought so, but actually it was not a good night at all.

It was a mere half an hour since I had slept when somebody knocked on the door like the boxing punches, proving calamitous for me. Oh no! what happened? Who was that rascal? I asked my room-mates with anger clearly visible on my face.

"It was Lucy asking all of us to gather in the hall," Softy replied back tensely.

"But why?," I asked him, totally confused.

"Our seniors wish to see all of us, dear...."

A little flash back….

Oh yes, engineering without ragging is incomplete. Lucy was a good friend of mine throughout my engineering days. In the starting phase, he was very simple and dedicated. But as the time passed, he did his makeover and got a typical local look. And that too with a lightly bearded face and the best sunglasses rented by one of our good local friends Saambha to impress a local girl. Whenever I saw both of them together in the corridor, I had a good laugh at Saambha's innocence. The very cunning Lucy was using Saambha to protect himself from any kind of local rage in the pursuance of his love.

However, after getting to know that Saambha was like any other guy coming from a different state and had nothing to do with manpower or anything else to protect him, Lucy started tormenting him and making fun of him in front of his friends. Saambha was far more innocent and of a friendlier spirit compared to Lucy.

So, everyone from our part of the hostel were all set to be ragged by the seniors and many of us were having no idea of what they were going to do with us. And I was again not thinking at all about the scene as usual.

Finally, the stage was all set for the ragging to begin. It all started with us forming a queue in front of the scary gang. We had to count ourselves alternately in Hindi and English. And in doing that many fumbled and were punished accordingly. After all, those "counting mistakes" were supposedly killing the precious time of our seniors, super seniors and the godfathers.

So many of us were soon singing unusual songs, or doing some bone-breaking exercises for our seniors, which were quite entertaining for them and for me as well until Teddy was called for his introduction.

"Hey you black beauty, come out of the queue," one

of the seniors called him out smugly.

I just managed to whisper in Teddy's ear to tell them "suck and run."

"Gone mad or what? They are our seniors. Just stay here. Next are you to be called... you dumb idiot," he whispered furiously and moved ahead

"It seems you have got a lot of attitude dear. It's clearly visible on your face. But, it's ok you will have no more attitude after all this. Introduce yourself," one of the godfathers with long hair and smart looks ordered with the clear intention of making fun of him. I too got ready to see what was going to happen to Teddy.

"Sir, this is me and it is my dream to be in the army one day to serve my country. I salute every army person leading from the front at the borders of my country."

"It's ok, stop," ordered the godfather while some lot of seniors were busy ragging other batch mates.

"So, if you wanted to join the Indian army, why are you here doing engineering? You should have given a good thought before you joined here," the godfather said, reminding Teddy of his mistake. It was a bit relaxing for me as well to know all that. Ragging was going smooth and relaxed, I thought, until the godfather ordered something unusual for Teddy to do.

"So, you wanted to join the army. Then, you must possess a physique like the armymen?," the godfather asked Teddy, standing proud in his group of friends.

"Yes you are right boss...what I have to do?" Teddy replied back to the godfather, sounding resigned.

"That is ok then. Show me your bravery. Just stay

here for some more time."

And then the godfather pointed something towards us in the queue which created a bit of uncertainty as to whether he was calling me or Softy or my other room-mates standing just ahead of me in the same queue.

The godfather picked out two of us for his plan; Softy and my other room-mate. And that was a bit relaxing for me as I was dropped for a while at least.

It was time for Teddy to show some bravery to the godfather. And we were having no idea what the godfather was going to do with Teddy and his samples from the queue. Everybody was shivering and filled with nervous excitement.

Move some ten metres away from here," the godfather instructed Teddy, mentally calculating the distance and showing his hand to Teddy like a traffic controller.

"Yes sir," Teddy complied without any questions. And I liked that attitude of Teddy.

"Now, you two guys come over here." Be quick you freshers," ordered the godfather pointing his index and the middle fingers to Softy and the room-mate. "Stand here in opposite direction."

And then in a very quick span of time the stage for the bravery show was all set for Teddy….

The two of them were standing in a geometric pose of 135 degrees, with their bums facing each other and their hands lifting free in air with very little space between them. The picture in front of me was getting clearer. They were looking like the female idols in a water park or like the statues placed at entrances in auspicious functions, welcoming guests. Watching their comical pose a little spark of laughter ignited within me...I just managed to control it by biting my tongue.

"Everyone's ready now for the drama?," asked the godfather merrily, rubbing his hands.

A very sick "yes sir" was the reply from the three participants. But the godfather was not satisfied. "Make it loud and clear you silly dumb freshers," he shouted, stretching his hands in anger.

YES SIRRRR...was the firm reply this time from the three of them.

"That's better! So Teddy, you have to run over from there and cross this hurdle in a single attempt," ordered the godfather pointing to the idols.

"Let's start now, on the count of three."

"It's 1...2...and 3...run, run baby run!"

Teddy with his firm attitude was on the run now, with his eyes sharp, looking for the aim. As he approached his maximum speed in the short distance and was about to cross the hurdle with his right leg up for the jump, he just mistimed the leap and collided with my room partners like a barmy elephant.

As a result, my two room-mates scattered in the two opposite directions like in the game of carom, when the striker hits two adjacent coins in the centre of the board at a single time and they go in different holes.

The three of them got wounded but I couldn't help chuckling at the comedy of it.

My laughter almost echoed in the hall, drawing the attention of the godfather.

"Very smart…what do you think of yourself?," he asked, walking towards me.

"No sir, it's not like that," I began earnestly, "It just broke out of my mouth. I am really sorry for it. I was…."

The godfather interrupted in between and said again, "You think you laugh well and you can laugh well on others' miserable situations. I am going to punish you for that severely; you won't be able to laugh any more on others. Just follow me," he said and moved away taking me with him.

As I followed him, the three victims made vulgar hand gestures at me. Softy showed me his middle finger, while Teddy and my other room-mate showed their hands like they were pumping down, grabbing something in their hand.

Anyways, I too showed them my both middle fingers, waving at them in the air, moving ahead with the godfather.

And when we reached the corner-most room of the hostel corridor, the godfather asked me to remain outside for a while and come inside only when asked to do so.

While I waited, I could listen to some mimicry sounds and dancing steps of my batch mates who were being ragged by the seniors. And after waiting outside for ten long minutes, two of my batch mates came out looking at me with recognition in their eyes. I introduced myself and shook hands with both, feeling proud within. These two guys later turned out to be the most caring friends of mine. The guy who was doing mimicry was Genie and the other dancing was Mini. Actually, they both are going to be the end and the cause of the story respectively....

"See you guys," I said entering into the room while they moved away.

As I entered the room, I saw something very interesting like a round-table conference happening on some very special issue. They were a group of ten or it's like, talking about the freshers and enjoying some of the incidences that had happened during ragging till then.

All of a sudden, a little fellow from their group saw me standing there at the door, and asked me, "Who are you dear? Why are you standing here?"

"I was told to follow him sir," I replied, pointing to the godfather. But the little fellow got furious over me, warning me not to show my fingers again to any of the seniors.

"It's ok sir, I am sorry, I'll take care not to repeat it," I said apologetically.

Now, it was the godfather's turn.

"With whose permission did you enter into the room?," he asked me harshly, taking me by surprise.

"No one's sir...you yourself told me to follow you. So, I came," I replied blandly.

"So what? If I would have moved in the middle of GT Road, would you have followed me there as well, you fool?," he snorted, his eyebrows climbing his forehead and pointing outside the window towards the national highway.

I didn't know really, whether he was advising me or asking or wanted me to do something else. So I decided not to reply believing that giving respect to my senior was my ultimate sense of duty.

"Ok introduce yourself," asked the little fellow sitting beside the godfather.

"No, you first go out and again come after taking permission," the godfather intervened. Like an obedient child, I moved out of the room.

Again while entering the room, I took a long breath and recalled my theory of relaxation– *have patience and be confident and the rest is going to be alright....* I knocked on the door and asked for their permission to let me come inside the room.

"Yeah sure, come in dear. You have paid to be in this great institution," said the little fellow with a little smile on his face and continued:

"Hey guys, have a look at his physique. It looks like something round. A very circular creature you are."

I took his words as a compliment and felt good as he was lenient on me.

"It's ok, you entered the room after taking permission but, who will wish all of us, your servant?"

"Oh... so sorry once again," I said and wished him a very good morning as it was already getting 1:30 am.

"Hey dude, I am not alone here. Wish everybody present in this room," the godfather ordered me.

"It's ok sir," I replied and started wishing every senior present in the room with my head down.

"It was very far from perfection...do me a favour; you just go outside and come back again with same commitments," ordered the godfather.

"Yes sir, sure." And I moved out and came back again following the same procedure, bowing to every senior with my greetings.

"It's not like that, you circular head," said the godfather again while coming up to me.

"You have to greet everyone present in this room like this," he said, and made me bow in front of them at bending at ninety degrees.

The position was killing me but I had no option but to oblige them.

"You are near to perfection, but not quite perfect. I made you do the things, now you repeat this whole process for all of us…will you?," the godfather asked, though it was more of an order.

"It's ok sir, I will," I said affirmatively also wanting to check that how many times they wanted me to do these silly things.

"It's me now…may I come in sir?," I asked for the permission looking at all of them and I felt great to observe that not all of them were able to have direct eye contact with me….

And as I got the permission, I bowed down and wished every senior expecting it to be the last time. I put in a lot of pressure on my head while standing up so that my eyes could look dark red, like I was in deep anger or I was tired of doing all that. Either heads or tails….

Unfortunately, the little fellow picked heads. "Ohh my God, you can have such looks as well. Have a look at your face, at the red circular hot-looking eyes…I can't believe your face," said the little fellow with a big smile on his face.

"You dirty fresher, you have ruined all the air here and it seems you have got a lot of temperature in you," the godfather remarked nastily and asked everyone to come out of the room.

Actually, while making my last ninety-degree bow to the little fellow, a very usual but unexpected sound had come to my ears, something like a fart from him only as he was sitting nearest to me. And the godfather blamed me for it! It was for this reason only that I wanted to leave and had made my head and the eyes red so I could avoid all the nonsense of the little fellow.

Now, the godfather took everybody outside the room into the ground, while the little fellow continued keeping the stupid smile on his face.

"Ok fine, you have lots of heat in you. Take complete ten rounds of this ground. It's cold outside and you will definitely feel better after doing that." The godfather said while liting a cigarette.

I agreed to his demands and started making rounds of the ground which was looking perfect for any budding athlete.

By the time I was into my fourth round, I thought such rounds would definitely make me an athlete if not an engineer. Also, I thought that if I continued to make rounds like that, they would keep making me run forever. So I pretended as if I would collapse. I fell down on the ground, although I still had some stamina left in me to complete all the rounds. And as the little fellow noticed that, they all rushed to me and took me over to the nearest bench.

"You alright?," the godfather asked, sounding genuinely concerned.

"Yes sir, aaaah, ouch!" I replied, showing my drowsiness with some premeditated extra efforts.

"Have some water," the little fellow said, offering a water bottle while he was having a super cool looking beer can in his other hand.

I grabbed the beer can rather, pretending as if I was mistaken in my drowsiness. Thankfully, my trick had worked.

"Thank you sir," I said. Although the beer can was of the little fellow, I thanked the godfather, wishing he would not carry out any more of his acts as I desperately wanted to sleep.

"It's ok dear, come, sit here with us," the godfather said kindly. Apparently, my playacting was having the desired effect on them.

"Ok sir fine, I am alright now, feeling much better," I said, looking at everyone standing making a cover around me.

They probably wanted to talk to me to ensure that I do not complain under any kind of anti-ragging regulations set by the institute.

"Ok now, enough with your physical exercise and all that...now tell me more about yourself like your habits," asked the little fellow while the godfather was busy giving horny looks to something on his mobile.

"Means what?," I asked him back, looking confused.

"Ok, do you drink hard or beer is enough for you? Do you smoke?," the little fellow asked.

"Ohh, I am always up for the parties; and drinking and smoking is all part of that. So, I do drink and smoke as well."

"And what about this?," the godfather asked me, rubbing his right thumb on to his left hand's palm.

"Ohh…tobacco!! Never sir, what are you saying?," I replied with a little smile, hiding my surprise.

"Ok now, just tell me the truth, how many girlfriends do you have?," the little fellow asked again.

"Sir, to be true, I have none," I replied, looking up in the sky watching a falling star.

"What are you saying? You don't have any girlfriends? I can't believe this. Why are you lying to me? Is there any problem? Look, we are not going to take away your girlfriend," the little fellow said, his questions multiplying.

"No way sir, it's not like that. Really, I don't have any girlfriends. And I don't lie," I clarified.

"Whatever… It's cool!!"

"Ok now, let's move," godfather told the little fellow while looking at me, "Look dear, you have the right potential, and you have the true confidence. I think you will move ahead in your life."

"Ok, you won't be ragged anymore by anyone, and don't hesitate to come to us if you have a problem. We are here to help you," the godfather said, even giving a pat on my back.

So, finally we exchanged a very sweet good night and

went off to our respective corridors.

While walking to my room, thoughts kept coming in my mind about the way I was ragged. It was nothing like any kind of embarrassment for me, to be honest. And to be honest again, I felt really proud to observe that I was the only student in my batch who was ragged so badly by our seniors.

Anyway, I developed my first official personal relations with my seniors. And I felt so good as if I had completed the whole of the coming assignments of the running semester. I felt really confident.

I reached my corridor and while moving towards my room, I decided to check on my friend Teddy. He was sleeping, so I didn't disturb him. Like most hosteliers Genie and Mini, whom I had met a short while ago, were awake. Good night friends!!

It was almost three in the morning by the time I entered my room. Every one else in the room was deep in sleep. I wished them good night too in a low voice and then finally fell on to my bed as if it was waiting for me. The whole of the day was so tiring that I didn't realize when I went into a deep and relaxing sleep.

The next morning, I started the day as usual with a "flake" lighting ceremony and went for the first duty of the day. Ohh… how relaxing that can be and that too with a cigarette puff and I continued with brushing my teeth after I got rid of my pressure and took a good bath. "Wow, what a good student I am, an ideal one." Such thoughts were coming in my mind as I successfully and confidently started my day. It was 9:30 a.m. and the other guys were still sleeping.

Suddenly, I heard the voice of Softy searching for someone like a culprit.

He asked me, “Was there somebody else in the room? What bad smell is this? Did you smoke?”

“Hey man stop! You will get tired asking so many questions. Yes I did smoke and nobody else was here.”

“You are a complete idiot; A pure wild man,” he ranted back some beauty of his own and I was enjoying the moment with my heart open thinking that the day will come when he will start smoking and again he will look for me, but this time for a lighter. Anyway, I moved ahead for my lectures.

I said, “See you later, until then, enjoy your day. All the very best to you, and a very cold good morning as well to keep you cool.”

So, after attending some daring lectures, we again moved to the cafeteria. It was me and Teddy again enjoying the lunch with the beautiful conversation but not like the previous night quarrelling.

“We are getting late, let's move for the lectures,” I told Teddy.

“Yeah sure, by the way whose lecture is this?,” he asked.

“It's again Narang's Information System. Be fast, come on,” I ordered him.

With firm determination, we started moving towards the lecture room to overcome the devil of Narang and to see what exactly he was made of.

The lecturer arrived with some files, a duster and a

marker in his hand. Wow, what was the personality he was having! Just looking at him for the first time itself was motivating. At the same time though my heart was pumping with some extra efforts, with the fear that I can be asked questions any time.

"It's 11:40. Level 0, multimedia students, attendance please."

And the lecturer started calling rolls of the 40 budding engineers. I felt proud thinking that calling by names was easier for Narang rather than calling roll numbers. It seemed as if it was the first time he was calling by roll numbers. I was about to raise my arm to give him a token of advice but restrained myself, thinking of my limitations towards a lecturer and that the teacher has to be respected at any place, any time and with no conditions applied. This was not my theory but of my father's.

Well, the second day of the module started with some exchange of knowledge between teacher and the students. I had a lucky escape as I was not asked any questions by the lecturer. On the other hand, it was too boring to see guys giving some diplomatic answers and making their hollow impression on the lecturer.

It was all going nice. Suddenly, the topic of the lecture got deviated from the subject as the lecturer got angry over something in the classroom.

He called out a girl and asked her unexpectedly, "Ok...you live in the girls' hostel?"

She replied, "Yes sir."

He continued, "So, what do you do when you have mosquitoes at night when you sleep?" "I mean... you have got the bedding from the management and the nets as well; you have the…etc…etc. so?"

The girl became quite nervous and started fidgeting so he asked her to sit down, assuring that everything was ok.

Actually, the lecturer was trying to joke on the fact that there was this guy in the class who was continuously sleeping for the past 15 minutes.

"You guys don't sleep at night... chatting, gaming and gossiping…and here is the result," he said, with his eyebrows raised. "Anyway, see you all the next time. All the best."

I think I was the only student who was mesmerized by his way of cracking the bad ones.

"I am impressed with Mr Narang. I think he has an ideal personality," I said to Teddy after the class ended.

"Just suck and run…Yes, he was good…but not the best," he replied me back with some sort of feelings.

I said, "He did ok…keep calm," with a smile on my face.

"See you tomorrow. Bye…."

Now I was moving ahead to my room with my backpack and feeling excited for nothing in particular. The excitement could have been for the chilled beer cans, I guess. Yes it was. And I went straight to the beer shop and bought two cans of super strong beer.

I was with my room-mates and the platform was all set for the first conflict in my college life, which I never meant to start.

"So, what you have to say dear friend Softy?," I asked

the leader with my eyes searching everyone's face and finding great expectations.

Softy replied on behalf of his group members, "Look, we don't need the makeover plans of what you do in the morning hours but man you can't have such wild behaviour. Yes, we can't take it. Personally I am unable to adjust with you and your smoke. It's problematic for me sometimes understanding you. So, either I quit or we all three are changing our rooms.

While I enjoyed every sip of my beer, I was a little astonished…by their way of presenting things. It was all bullshit and nothing more than that.

"So, no compromises from either side," I said.

"Ok, give me some time. It's quite a possibility; I would quit my bad habits."

At that time I knew I was never going to quit smoking at least, but convinced them in good favour.

It was all very confusing, but I left for dinner fixing the virus within. After dinner I went to bed playing my sweet songs and woke up early the next morning as usual, even though I did not have a sound sleep.

I had some nightmares, in which I saw myself as a man wandering in a jungle, that too wearing only banana leaves searching for nothing. "Ohh no…am I really a wild man?," I thought.

I was getting ready for the lectures. As I was about to leave for the day, suddenly I thought–I can't be the victim of words.

I just looked at the clock, and relaxed for a while. I waited for about 15 minutes till the clock ticked to

9:55 a.m. The best part was that the other guys were still asleep. And I was in a hurry. Thanks to the management, for they had provided attached toilets. I went straight to the shit pot taking with me something around 10-15 old newspapers and cut them into pieces.

I just implemented my idea, though it was completely rubbish. But, I knew my action was better than their culprit words.

I filled in the shit pot with those newspaper pieces congesting whole of the system, and covered it for their surprise.

So, I was finally done. Then I wished my room-mates a very pleasant good morning, urging them to watch the clock and get up quickly and left for my lectures.

At the lunch time, it was me and Teddy enjoying our food with some fuzzy drinks analysing some good upcoming movie trailers. At the same time...something happened unexpectedly to me like some evil force pounced on me. Yeah! it was Softy with his expected outburst.

I said–"Welcome you. What will you have sir?," pretending as if I had done nothing.

"So what do you think of yourself?," Softy asked me.

"If you had to ask me only this...you could have sent somebody else. Why is the leader so much bothered about what I think of myself. Anyway, I am just a zero. So?"

"Yes we were right. You are such an idiot...you are really a wild man and for your smart ways we missed our lectures," Softy replied with a bang.

But, I was ready for that to happen. "I said it's ok

man, stay cool. Don't lose your temper."

"You just shove away," he said again.

Teddy intervened and lashed out at Softy, "You be in your limits, to whom are you talking in such a way? He happens to be my good friend and I damn care for my friends…is that ok with you?"

"No way Teddy, you better stay out of this…I can handle it," I requested Teddy and then continued further with my words.

"Hey Softy, man you have become serious on this issue…you know what, you guys missed your lectures but I couldn't sleep the whole night."

"Look, that was entirely your problem. What can I do in that?," Softy said.

It was time for me to conclude this drama.

"Ok, I was damn right in doing what I did today. But, I never did such an act before…it was you guys calling me the wild man…and don't you think you have paid for that by just missing your lectures only?" I defended my act.

"It's over now. I am leaving that room," Softy replied emotionally.

"No, neither you nor others would leave. I shall find another room," I said and continued with a question for Softy.

"How many platforms are there at the New Delhi railway station?"

Softy replied, "What does this have to do with anything? I don't know."

"No, you must know that there are 16 platforms. And it's only a matter of time which platform is free or open to arrive or depart from. I mean you guys are good friends; you need not sacrifice for a stupid person like me. I would leave by the night. See you at that time."

Now, that's what I call the real nailing of ears.... Teddy intervened in between with a big smile on his face which made me break into a fit of laughter.

It was over then and Softy just went back shaking his head.

And that led to the end of my first encounter putting me on an emotional low.

But it was really disappointing from my side to do a breakup with friends. It was really tough.

Anyway, I realized my fault and shifted to the adjacent room A-24 with my luggage with the authorized approval from the administration.

***

Wiping tears

I shifted to my new room allotted by the administration trying to forget my first encounter. It was all good and it started with a very formal introduction. First one was a very out of the place kind of a guy. So, I named him Oops. I shook hands with him with a very strange feeling of a conspiracy in the air.

Next one was Pastry. I named him so because of his looks; he was really a handsome guy with the aroma of Delhi that any girl would have loved to have. "Hello to you too sir," I greeted him, extending my hand. Embarrassed, he realized what he was supposed to do.

"Ohh… hi dear!!" he said while removing his headphones.

We both shook hands with foolish smiles on our faces. And the best part was that I liked his attitude, he was a very cool guy. "I am going to enjoy my studies and the coming days," I thought.

The third one was Lingo, a man with his own dreams. "Lingo," because of his very informal way of communicating; a very intelligent, hard-working chap with the ambition of becoming Enrique one day.

The days passed. I had got the fourth corner of the room. Soon, I also found caption for my cupboard as the other three had their own–

For Lingo, it was–life sucks, the only devil of APIIT.

For Pastry, it said–life is calling, where are you! Keep walking–so get lost.

For Oops, it was like I think well when I am drunk, I am born to make you happy….

My caption for my cupboard read–"life is a party, go have a blast…in hole."

Everything was going perfect. All of us were enjoying superbly. Any time partying, making fun of each other and outings (of course) with girlfriends.

Meanwhile, we covered all our assignments, internals and quizzes with ease, but invariably we would submit assignments in the last hour which always proved to be a real thrilling experience for us.

Suddenly, the bells started ringing for the final examinations. That was devastating for all of us. Well, I was relaxed for the externals. But, there was one module which kept giving me shivers. Although I had learnt A for apple, B for boy in my childhood, I never expected C for language. And throughout my 1st semester, could never understand the concepts of this programming language.

Problem solving and programme designing using a bull shit programming language. Throughout my engineering I really hated being a coder.

Everyone was out hanging on the notice board for

the results. I was there too, with my heart pumping in the extremely tense conditions. It was a moment of deep grief, I had failed. It hurt more when friends like Pastry and Teddy had managed to pass.

The stupid day concluded on a very sad note for me. And I reached my room without uttering a single word to anyone.

In the evening, others were in the room. And I was busy with my computer, playing racing games. In between, Pastry said, "How come you failed dear?"

"Ohh yes...I failed. But, I have the re-sit for that as well. Hopefully, I will overcome the situation then," I managed to reply anyhow.

"Of course, my dear friend! But you are still a failure until then." This baseless reply of Pastry really blew me up. Somehow I just managed to control my anger and went for dinner. I tried to keep myself busy after that.

"What happened friends?," I asked everyone, returning to my room.

"Nothing much; Pastry was trying to change your BIOS password but could not succeed and now your computer is not starting," Oops replied.

Exactly that was the time when I very nearly busted, but refused to start a revolt against Pastry. "So Mr Pastry you like doing experiments. It's good, as you must have passed your exams doing such silly experiments," I told him acidly.

Meanwhile, Oops and Lingo intervened, in fear of my second encounter.

I went outside the room for a good smoke. And while

I was about to complete my packet of cigarettes, Pastry came up.

"Hey Golu, I am really sorry friend. I have realized that I was making fun of you. I am extremely sorry for that nonsense."

"It's cool. No issues," I said.

"Will you give me one flake, I forgot to have any today? You can at least afford to spare one," Pastry requested me.

"Who says smoking is injurious to health? When it brings people closer," with a stupid smile on my face, I replied to Pastry offering him a cigarette. It's ok."

In between those silly moments I was having some officially unwanted but friendly tears. But I wiped them before Pastry arrived there for a cigarette, not giving him another reason to call me a failure.

Anyway, it was all part of life. That's why for me life has always been learning things to implement for enjoyment; learnt here, implemented somewhere. After that, Pastry and I remained good friends forever.

Cheers to friendship..!!

***

The red monk night

So, we all were having a good time really. Apart from studies, we partied hard. Actually, I put on my study books in a reservation quota for a while. Thanks to the government for providing such a nice concept of quotas. We could put nearly anything in that.

Further, Oops birthday was approaching, with only two days left. So, we all geared up for that. And in the process of celebrations, we prepared some of our pet tools to hammer his bum till it needed wiring.

Overall, Oops was a good guy, an intelligent student as well. But, his desire of knowing everything included interfering in others' personal matters.

Anyway, we carried out the party when the big night arrived. Oops was ready to execute his part; he bought four bottles of Red Monk rum with snacks and salads…of which I loved salads the most.

So, finally we met at a nearby drunk yard. The clock struck 12, it was midnight and we just banged his ass and almost converted it into *kulfi faaluda*. After all, we had our great pet tools (our leather shoes in pillow covers). And finally the auspicious cake-cutting ceremony which was held with the slogans shouted aloud like– "long live Oops."

Now, only we four room-mates were left in the drunk yard. And the bottles were about to be opened. Oops was busy receiving calls of best wishes from his admirers. Just when we were all ready his phone rang with a very cute ring tone dedicated to his girlfriend.

"Ohh no…not again..!" I wailed while Pastry and Lingo were busy decorating the things on the table.

I observed that Oops was busy collecting some unrealistic sympathy from his girlfriend. I managed to overhear some of the words uttered by Oops that were, "Ohh no dear it is so painful they have almost double cracked me."

Here, I got the chance and shouted loudly- "Ohh really, you will have to come here and massage his bums dear, madam girlfriend." These words resulted in a laughing riot for Lingo and Pastry. And I just escaped the situation by tuning the music louder. Actually, I was showing some sympathy to the boys who were alone having no girlfriends. I maintained the true spirit of friendship while doing that.

"So, let's start now," I urged to all, after Oops finished his never-ending conversation.

Our first peg was dedicated to Oops of course, but what about those victims of terrorism? I added pointing to the people killed in the recent attacks, so we drank to them as well pointing our faces and glasses upward in the sky. Actually, we kept two minutes of silence for those who were killed. Finally, cheers was the word and we four engulfed our first peg....

"Ohh... it tastes good. Thanks for this party. You know what Oops, from my side you have got six months of my life. I am dedicating my six months to you," said Pastry in gratitude. Lingo and Pastry kept thanking Oops, while I enjoyed my drink.

I said, "Ohh really friends, Oops would take those days which include your wedding nights for granted. So better be careful with your words," I said laughing like Ravan, as a result of which a nearby sleeping dog woke up and shifted itself to another spot for a good sleep.

We all laughed and welcomed two other guys from software branch named Jackie and Chocos. "Come on friends you are most welcome here; let's enjoy; it's Oops' birthday today."

"Yeah we know that, that's why we are here...," Chocos said while congratulating Oops.

As time was passing, we were getting tightened by the drinks. Now Oops had to say something to me, "So, you have my slippers today? You shouldn't have dear, I just purchased them today only and you have ruined them."

"Ohh Oops, leave it...I would pay you 300 bucks for your slippers," I replied, assuming that to be the price of those silly slippers.

"Three hundred...it's for double the cost you have assumed dear...."

"Whatever that be. Hey listen, what do you want? Why don't you put me on your feet and make your slippers sit over here on this chair."

"It's ok man, enjoy the party," Oops replied, trying

for a makeover.

And then in between all that, someone's romantic ring tone could be heard. It was Chocos as if he was waiting for that call from his girlfriend.

"Excuse me friends," he said, while standing up from his chair and taking out his mobile from his pocket.

"Hey, when you didn't want to attend this party then why did you come?," Pastry asked him back with some blend of anger in his mood.

"It's ok dear…come soon," I asked Chocos to come back as soon as possible and Chocos became invisible in no time.

So, the party picked up with some hard pegs and we started losing control. As a result, something unusual had to happen for sure; it was around 01:45 am already.

I stood up pushing my chair.

"Anybody coming? I am out for the,..," I gestured with my left hand's little finger to everyone present there.

"Yes I am," confirmed Jackie, raising his hand, while remaining three stayed there.

"Let's move…!" We agreed.

While we were still at it, Jackie and I started gossiping about the slippers, Oops' poor attitude and his lack of spirit. Ohh really, it was too much, said Jackie.

"It's ok man, leave all this and be fast, we have to complete that last bottle as well," I said.

"Ohh my goodness, the stage ahead is going to be the eventual one and Jackie you better pardon me for my act…."

I was so drunk that I had lost my control somewhere like in the hell....

Actually, I was standing behind Jackie. But, assuming that, I was standing parallel to Jackie, I was pissing on Jackie's leg. Ohh my goodness!!

"You are nothing less than a duffer," Jackie shouted.

"I am sorry man," I said while running somewhere to escape his fury, but I landed in a nearby puddle which was deep enough to engulf my left leg till its knees.

At the same time, I was applying my second leg into the mud to get out. But, it was really thick and heavy. As a result, I trapped both my legs in that. After trying hard, I managed to take out one of the slippers with my hand, and shouted for the help. Pastry and Lingo came running while Jackie was still angry and showed no concern for me. Pastry and Lingo took me out of that hell though they themselves were heavily drunk.

So, Lingo in action now... when I told him that one of the slippers was still trapped in the mud, he started searching for a stick, but, failed to find any. Then Lingo, in his real unconscious state of mind, anyhow found one tea spoon from somewhere and with that spoon started scooping out the mud from the exact region to find the slipper.

"He is drunk man...he is out of his mind now," Pastry said, with his thumbs in his mouth." And I was amazingly grateful watching Lingo whirling his spoon into a little more than a foot deep-mud to find out Oops' slipper.

"Everybody out now, let's wrap up this party...let's

move back. It's around 3 am," Oops urged us all.

Until then I had washed my hands and legs, and Jackie was busy convincing Lingo. "Look man–we have told the owner of this drunk yard to return back the slipper when he gets it. Is that ok?," Jackie managed to convince Lingo and requested him to move inside.

The rhythm soon shifted to our very special room. Everybody was in now. Oops was about to sleep and I asked, "Who would like to conquer the last frontier?," looking at everybody with hope after taking a good bath. While Jackie rejected the offer, Lingo and Pastry supported me for the good cause.

Lingo was completely out until then. It was me and Pastry who finished the bottle. None of us was in a mood to sleep. Pastry lost his emotions and started begging sorry for his calling me a failure and that too continuously for an hour, rather unexpectedly.

"Hey man look, I don't have any issue with you. I don't even remember it. It's cool from my side."

"No, do you recognize me as your friend?," Pastry asked me with lots of emotions in his voice.

"Yes man of course...you know what, you are here... I mean, I keep you here...," I said without concluding my sentence and pointing my finger to my heart.

"But where?," Pastry asked me.

"Here man...in front of....!"

"What in front of... ohh in your heart?," he asked me again with frustration and hope.

"Not exactly there. But, here...in front of the centre of the heart," I replied convincingly.

"Ohh thanks a lot. Good I like that," Pastry said while I supported him to bed thinking about something. Even I had started feeling sleepy and so went to bed.

But, the story was not over yet.

Suddenly, sounds of coughing and vomiting came to my ears. I really felt as if I was vomiting somewhere and ran to the wash basin which was already occupied by Lingo. Actually, Lingo had the habit of putting his first three fingers deep into his throat and vomit to settle his mind whenever he drunk.

"Open the door Lingo!" I urged, covering my mouth with a hanky, feeling the nausea.

"Yeah sure, it's ok now. Feeling fine now," Lingo was about to open the door uttering those words. But, I ran short of time and couldn't control the tsunami within my stomach. As a result of that, as Lingo opened the door, I completely vomited on his beautiful sweater. Ohh no…that was the real outburst on him. It was all like the water coming out from a tube-well.

"You can't do this to me," he said, getting annoyed.

"I am sorry, leave this here only…we will see it next day. Good night," I said and finally rushed to bed. Really, pissing on Jackie's leg, trapping Oops' brand new slippers in mud and vomiting on to Lingo's beautiful sweater was like too much for me.

I felt guilty of my sins. But, thoughts automatically came in my mind about Chocos, one of our good friends, how girlfriends were more important to him and how he did not bother to stay in the party thrown for all of us.

Anyway, a beautiful good night I said to myself,

although, the clock was already showing the start of the sunshine.... The next morning, I had to narrate this whole story to as many people as possible to finish my laughter riot. Thanks to Oops for such a nice party.

As the time passed, we enjoyed every bit of our college life.

Pastry managed to bring his maternal uncle's scooter from Rohtak, as per a deal between him and Oops. According to that agreement between them, Pastry had to bring that scooter and Oops had to fill up the petrol tank every alternate day.

This, however, never happened.

Whenever Oops wanted to use that scooter, he would fill up the tank. But, he refused to do it otherwise.

And that made Oops not so trustworthy for Pastry and created the root for his separation from the agreement.

Pastry finally decided not to use his scooter anymore, not even for his personal use and kept it in the hostel garage.

Not only this, Oops never allowed us to use his personal things, not even his desktop. And contrary to that, whenever he required others' help he would ask or it without any hesitation.

This created some uncomfort in the room. As I was observing all this, I also felt his introvert and self-centered behaviour maynot be healthy for the relationship we all shared till now.

Anyway, we never shared our opinions amongst oursleves although each one of us was finding his behaviour weired and had decided to stay away from him.

***

The warden's psychotherapy

It was already the and of the first year. Holi was round the corner. So everybody was gearing up for the celebrations.

We dug out a space outside the park; something like a mud pit. We carved out as much land so that one could easily be drowned vertically in the pit. It was filled with a thick paste of mud only; no colours or water.

We also managed to have an open air DJ of our own, which involved having four big loudspeakers like any of the surround sound system in a closed room, giving the same effects. After that was done, our next mission was to prepare the green thunder *desi* drink known superbly as *thandai*, free for everyone.

So, the day came and we were all set to celebrate the festival with excitement peaking on everyone's face. Everybody was on the stage dancing on famous track numbers dedicated to Holi.

We just started throwing each other into the mud taking quick snaps of the thrown guys, and having the taste of *thandai*.

Everyone was busy celebrating the festival with extreme joy....

Suddenly, one familiar voice rang out loud in between us. It was Oops calling for everyone in a very surprised state of mind as if he had seen something very unrealistic in between the celebrations....

"Who the hell are these guys?," Oops said, sounding perplexed.

And everyone started throwing some hard mud onto them so that they could remain out of the celebrations, as they were the outsiders and were thus uninvited guests.

Actually, those two guys were the laterals, who just came there to check out the atmosphere in our hostel.

Out of the two, one was having a moustache, coming out directly from his nose, and merging with the beard. Also, the thick smoke coming out of his mouth was giving him a very special, dynamic and a traditional look. I immediately named him 'The Holy Man.'

Other one was much taller than 'The Holy Man'; in fact, much-much taller than me too. Having a gigantic physique with a killer's edge in his looks and a semi French beard, without his moustache were all making him look like a *desi* wolverine. And thus I named him 'Kapala.'

"Everybody, please stop," I urged everyone not to throw mud on them without first having a introduction from them.

"Yeah sure." Genie intervened and asked me to talk to them.

"Sure, let's go."

Genie and I moved ahead to talk to them without any

hesitation in our mind, while others kept celebrating.

I offered my hand in friendship to 'Kapala'.

"Hi... I am Golu." I told him while looking at Genie, which got him in some very deep conversation with 'The Holy Man'....

"Hi...are you getting me?," I repeated.

"K...", the only letter, he replied.

I said hi again, offering my hand in friendship.

"K...?," He again replied unusually, which I was unable to understand. I wondered if he was stammering or something...but actually, he was replying in his typical pastoral tongue.

Then, the 'Holy Man' came forward and whispered something in Kapala's ear.

And perhaps he got it this time and he too offered his hand to me for friendship.

Genie and I welcomed the two to the Holi celebrations and threw both of them into the mud.

Soon we realised they had all good intentions and a clear heart. It was lovely making new friends.

The celebration continued with extreme joy and with the making of memories that would last a life time.

After taking the weekend off for rest, we started back with our classes recalling those memorable moments of the Holi celebrations.

We came to know from the notice board that the running week was going to be full of sports events. No sooner did the students get the very good piece of news, long hours of practice became the order of the day. Laptops and books, it appeared had just gone missing for a week.

I too wanted to play cricket for my multimedia team, but the main hurdle between my playing and selection was none other than Saambha. He presented himself as an all-rounder during the team meetings but thankfully our captain did not feel very confident of him after having a look at his batting and bowling. I was happy as it improved my chances of being included in the team.

I took the opportunity and recalled my excellence in the street cricket. I managed to present myself as a better option and got selected in the playing eleven.

So the stage was all set for the first cricket match of the sports week and it was Multimedia Vs Computing of the same batch.

The result of the toss was exciting. Our captain won and elected to bat first.

I went as an opener to face the first ball of the innings. The first ball pitched outside the off stump but swung back inside the main line forcing me into a well judged leave with my bat up above the shoulders, giving a perfect cricketing pose.

The second ball came nicely on to the bat and I just played a perfect straight drive resulting in a classic four that received a huge round of applause from the crowd.

But after that, the third ball came as a perfect, sharp yorker and I was clean bowled.

The bad timing of my dismissal compelled me to think whether I should play cricket again. I decided to take retirement from the game . And just when I was about to express my decision to the captain, Saambha gestured with his middle fingers, and said, “Over with your game baby?"

"Yeah, got a sharp yorker and was clean bowled," I replied, taking off my pads.

"Now you just tell me one thing; when you did not know how to face yorkers, why did you go to open the innings?" Saambha asked me again, tossing a ball in his hand.

This was the time when I realized how difficult it must be for the cricketers to explain things to the media when things go wrong.

"Anyway, it was my captain's decision and it's because I did not practise that I could not perform at the centre," I said, trying to clarify my situation.

I noticed Saambha was leaving no stone unturned to malign my sportsmanship spirit among others present there. He wanted the girls sitting around to laugh at my performance and, to some extent, he succeeded too. I could only wish him all the best for he was going to substitute me in the next innings. I knew I had performed poorly.

Anyway, we managed a very good total of 160 for the loss of seven wickets in 20 overs, thanks to some fabulous performances by our captain, who was a professional cricketer from Hyderabad and another stylish batsman from Kolkata.

In the next innings, as I had already decided not to play cricket anymore, I sat in the stands cheering for my team.

As the finish of the game approached, the scores stood like this-

Multimedia: 160/7

Computing: 150/9…

This meant, team Computing required 11 more runs to win the match with just one wicket in hand and the last five balls remaining.

But the problem was a bulky middle order batsman who was only hitting huge sixes and fours. He was looking really desperate to win the match for his team. But he had benefitted from an unfair decision given by the umpire in his favour.

Now, the last two balls remained, and they still required four more runs to win the match.

As the bowler was about to take his long run up to bowl, I thought "to hell with the sportsmanship" and shouted aloud, "Hey you batsmen, you are clean bowled now on this ball," compelling the batsmen to look at me before he could play his shot. And that did it. I succeeded as my idea clicked in breaking his concentration and he was clean bowled by a devastating block hole yorker….

We won the match finally by four runs which was quite satisfying for me.

"What was he telling you?," Genie, Kapala and the 'Holy Man' came together and asked me.

"It's ok dear, just take care of Saambha," I replied, patting Holy Man's back.

They were all angry on the way Saambha tried to tarnish my image in front of a huge crowd.

"Ok now, let's move," the 'Holy Man' ordered the rest and they moved ahead and became invisible as complete darkness descended.

The next day, everyone was discussing Saambha's

Orkut caption which said, "Soon I am going to delete my account," and everyone started questioning Saambha. Kapala, Genie and the 'Holy Man' too made desperate attempts to show that they were concerned to know why he had decided to delete his orkut account.

"Delete my Orkut account? What are you guys saying I have no idea," Saambha replied, looking totally surprised.

Later, did I come to know that it was actually the doing of the 'Holy Man', Kapala and Genie, who had made a fake profile of Saambha in order to teach him a lesson for trying to malign my image.

The next day, the same unexpected phenomenon happened. One more fake profile of Saambha read –"My name is Saambha, and I am not Lucy's servant."

The caption was making a close observation of the Lucy-Saambha close friendship.

This time Saambha approached me and asked for my help in getting rid of all the fake creations. I referred him to Lucy suggesting that Lucy might know something about it.

Although Lucy too was equally involved, he referred Saambha to the three actual creators of the fake profiles.

The three of them convinced Saambha that once they get to know they would definitely inform him, which provided Saambha with a lot of pseudo relaxation.

But the next day, the same thing recurred. This time his fake profile's caption stated, "My name is Saambha and I am a fool." Saambha was furious. He almost wanted to kill everyone out there. He begged everyone to tell him who were the actual creators of the fake profiles on Orkut.

But, instead of telling him the truth, everybody started shouting, "long live the Saambha…!"

Saambha finally went to the ground and shouted, "Noooooo…my father has given me a name, and my name is not Saambha!"

Later, I met him and made him understand the what and why of things that had caused him so much anguish. I explained it to him that his friends were annoyed with him for settling his score in public and wanted to teach him a lesson. I told him politely that he should have had decency to behave in public. He, thankfully, did not react.

The life was back to normal. One fine night, around 11:45 we all including Teddy, Genie, Kapala, the 'Holy Man' and I were returned from a wedding party as unwanted guests. The warden too did not allow us to enter the campus. He called our parents and all hell broke loose.

The issue was blown out of the proportion. We discussed the issue with our seniors and came to know about his psycho behavior towards students which was hard to digest to all of us….

Genie got an idea. He made duplicate keys using toilet soap impressions. And after observing the situation, we entered the warden's room.

"So, what are we up to?" Genie asked, while having a close look at the room with his rotating eyes.

"One thing for sure…," I said.

"What?," he asked me again, looking at Teddy.

"Don't ask questions, hold up this cot," I instructed

him, pointing towards the only bedding present in that room at the corner.

"Ok, now what?" Teddy and Genie asked, holding up the cot.

"Now, bring this cot here," I said, pointing my fingers to the centre of the room.

So the only cot was kept in the centre of the room. And after that, every other stuff present in the room was kept on that cot. It was all done to seriously indicate to the warden that 'your time is over now…stay away from any phone calls to students' parents….

"Let's move now," Genie asked both of us as the time was approaching for the warden's entry into his room.

"One more minute."

I just took the bucket and splashed some two three rounds of that bucket full of water on the floor.

"Yes, that's it now…let's move," I led Genie and Teddy out of the room.

The next day, we were all eagerly waiting for any reaction. The warden looked irritated. Without making fuss of it he ordered a change in the physical appearance of his room. The entry to his room was now walled and the door now opened on the opposite side so that the guards could keep a better vigil on it.

"Not much impact, it seems our move was not enough for him… let's plan something more grave," Genie said. We planned to wait for a week and then strike.

"Ok... the night of the conspiracy has arrived," Teddy asked us to gear up.

We moved to the warden's room. He was sleeping.

"Let's switch off the power supply to this part of the hostel and make it dark," Teddy said.

The three of us went straight to the main power supply box and after lowering down and fixing down the main switch to the same status by cementing that tightly, we returned to the warden's room. But in the way someone shouted loudly, "Who is there?"

"Shit, it's the guard's voice," Genie alerted us, hearing the unexpected but known voice of the guard.

"Who is this and what is happening here?," the guard asked us all, focusing his torch light on our faces.

"Ohh…Mr guard how are you?," Genie came to the rescue of all and presented himself in the best friendly manner to the guard.

"Yes, I am fine… but what is going on here?," he asked suspiciously.

"Hey, nothing like what you are thinking…we were just checking out the power supply," Teddy said, trying to sound as convincing as possible.

And there happened the mistake and the guard moved ahead to the power box, while he said all of us to stay there only. We couldn't escape from the situation as the power box was very near and he had identified us all.

"What is this? You guys have jammed the main switch! I am going to complain to the administration about all that has happened here."

"Ohh you think too much... it happens here," I said to the guard who was quite young.

"You look very smart in your cap and this baseball stick in your hand, just like the foreign cops in Hollywood movies," I said in order to convince him for a while to just shut up his mouth.

"Ohh really, is that so?"

My flattery seemed to have worked. He was overwhelmed and thought he actually looked like a Hollywood star.

"Yes you look like a Hollywood star. But, one thing is missing in your great personality." I involved him in a conversation so that it could distract him from the real issue.

"One whisky bottle in your hand," I cleared his doubt.

"Is that so?," he again asked me proudly touching his collar.

"Sure, I have one bottle, never mind that's empty. But, you will look amazingly smart with a whisky bottle in your one hand and the base ball stick in another."

"Teddy, will you please get that empty bottle for this gentleman," I asked Teddy, while whispering something in his ear. Teddy went away to his room.

We were almost done with the trap for that stupid guard.

"Ok, hold this bottle in your hand," I told him while Genie handed over that not so empty whisky bottle to the guard.

"Teddy, now bring out your new digital camera and be ready," I urged Teddy to bring out his camera from his cupboard and to be ready for the coming moment for the beautiful snaps.

Teddy clicked the cam, and started praising the guard,

"Look how smart you are looking in this picture."

"Ohh really!"

"But, your looks would have been much better had your lips touched this bottle," I told the guard while trying to finally trap him.

And the guard agreed to my point.

And he started licking the bottle and now Teddy was all set to click his digital camera for the last time…

"No way!! This has to be not like this, you are not playing a flute. Do it like the cops in style." Teddy said to the guard after clicking the camera and not getting the perfect snap.

"Ok now, are you ready?" Teddy asked.

"Yes sir… I am ready," the guard confirmed for Teddy to click, holding the bottle straight up in the air.

"Here you go now."

"In hell…," I finished, while taking the camera from Teddy.

"Ok now, you do your duty while drinking whisky… how can you put at risk the life and properties of these future engineers…?" I asked him while pointing my fingers towards the hostel rooms.

"What are you saying?, I am unable to understand."

"I am not saying anything to you. But, this smart-looking snap of yours is saying everything"

The guard now understood what we did to him….

"Look, I am sorry…please don't tell anybody…," he pleaded.

"Yes, we won't tell…if you promise us not to tell anyone, about anything that is going to happen tonight," Genie said, vaguely describing the situation to the guard.

"Ok, I won't, be assured about that...but, please don't tell anybody about this snap...," the guard said, looking fearfully at Teddy's digital camera.

"Ok, be assured from our side as well...but, if in case, this night's happenings are disclosed, we won't take much time in sending this snap to the administration. And you know better, what will happen to you after that," Teddy warned the guard.

"It's ok, I promise, I won't tell anybody. Let me go now," the guard assured us all and left the place.

"Ok now, let's proceed with planning," Genie said.

We moved ahead to the warden's door and checked if he was sleeping... we heaved a sigh of relief after we found him in deep sleep, snoring loudly.

After observing the situation out there, I told Teddy to bring out the pipeline that was connected to the water supply knob.

"Ok, let's start now," I asked everyone, holding up the water pipeline in my hand.

I extended the pipeline directly into the warden's room through the narrow space between the door and the floor.

Teddy came with wet cement in his hand and then we fixed that pipeline tightly in that place.

After that, I switched on the water knob, so that the water could smoothly flow into the warden's room. We managed to make sure that the water flowing inside could not come out.

Now, after waiting for some time, Genie came , "ok, it's my turn now...."

And in a very surprising act, he locked the warden's room from outside, trapping him inside.

And then, we ran out of that place shouting and creating noise, having winning smiles on our faces.

Now, the warden woke up listening to the noise coming inside his lonely room and while he tried to check out, he found himself locked into the room....

Meanwhile, almost everyone in the hostel came out in front of the warden's room. The power was still off and the warden was calling the guard frantically.

Taking advantage of darkness, everyone of us covered with a blanket, started shouting and making scary sounds...even some started pelting slippers, shoes...even spoons and plates onto the door and the windows of the warden's room.

The guard came, secretly giving a trustworthy smile to the three of us. We all rushed back to the our respective rooms, as the guard tried to break open the warden's room. Teddy offered him a good cigarette to puff for the night.

By next day evening, we came to know that the warden had been transferred to some other department of the administration.

After the mission was accomplished, started planning about how to rag our coming juniors. This was the most exciting time of the year. In a few days we were going to become seniors.

Bell rang again for the externals...and each one of us managed to clear our exams; me including...

***

The life ahead

It was the second year of engineering and each one of us was looking fresh, full of excitement, having a good amount of confidence on our faces after returning to college life.

Many of us were getting our ears pierced, hair straightened, tattoos and many other stylish changes in our looks to give a cool, scary look to the freshers. But the Supreme Court played a spoilsport. It directed the universities to ban ragging. Our college too issued anti-ragging norms. These were boring and heart-breaking for many of us.

Meanwhile, Genie and I had some introductory sessions with our juniors.

I was difficult to control our feelings and something happened in violation of the anti-ragging rules specified by the college authorities, which led to the expulsion of some of our good friends from the institute. We decided not to give a customary party to our juniors.

But we grew quite comfortable with some freshers, making good friends with them. We didn't even realize that it was already three months since we had become seniors.

We were all moving ahead with our academics. But at the same time, one stupid plot was waiting for one of my close friends.

It was Chaman's birthday. Genie and I were in no mood to attend the party because of his notorious character. He was a total jump start character and that's why we never had a good relationship with him.

To escape the party, I and Genie set out for dinner and a beer to a nearby restaurant. While I ordered a chilled beer can for myself and dinner for Genie, there was big shock awaiting us. Chaman entered the restaurant.

We tried to avoid him and started thinking about how to escape from the situation. As he was our batch-mate, there was no escaping him. He insisted that we attend his party.

"Genie, do you remember what happened at his party last year?" I asked Genie,

"Yes, that boy is still in pain from his broken leg. It was a terrible party," Genie replied, with his one eye closed and his face moving up and down.

Chaman had on his last birthday party pushed a serving boy from the first floor of the building. Although the guy was saved because of the timely treatment, he couldn't recover completely from his fractured leg.

While Genie was enjoying his dinner and I my beer, Chaman came and ordered:

"Come on guys, let's move for the party, it's about to start."

Genie looked at me and signalled that I must say no....

"No, I can't come to your party today. I am sorry dear, I have pain in my stomach...and that's why I am having a beer and not my dinner this night as you can see," I replied, making him look at the table already full of beer bottles, tandoori chicken, salads and a vegetarian plate for Genie.

"No way... you guys are coming... I don't know anything," Chaman again said, this time with his eyebrows about to touch each other.

While entering the party room, I found one more excuse but not like the previous one.

There were more than 40 guys at the party, including our batch-mates, juniors and even seniors.

"Party with these guys and here?...I can't believe this. I do not know them...no way, I am going back to my room, let's move Genie." I made a genuine excuse to Chaman as we desperately didn't want to be a part of that party.

"So, if you two are not coming to my party then it's over," Chaman replied looking at those present there. He called out his guests as if he was truly calling off the party, before it even started. "Let's move in," Genie said, afraid of the scene that was being created by Chaman.

Now, at this point of writing, I must confess that describing whole of the content about what exactly happened that night would only add to the humiliation of that unspecified character in the story. I wish I could erase that part of my life. So, all I can do is to offer my deeper apologies for that innocent character from every one of us present in that black night birthday party.

The next morning was catastrophic for some of us present in that party.

Genie and Chaman were prohibited from using the hostel facilities anymore and were ordered to vacate the hostel with immediate effect.

Genie was barred from providing the cell number to our seniors and Chaman for provoking our seniors to make a call to that unspecified character in a very unconscious state of mind.

At the same time one of our seniors was imposed with a whooping fine of Rs 10,000 for making a call to that unspecified character and using bad words.

But, it was only Genie and I , who knew that only I was responsible for those acts of shame.

The next day after the declaration of punishment for the horrifying act, I also came to know that back in the hostel there was a heated argument over Pastry's scooter between Oops and Pastry.

In fact, Pastry and Lingo decided to part ways with Oops and approached me to stay with them outside the hostel in any residential area nearby.

I said ok to them.

"So, should we forward our applications to the administration?," Pastry and Lingo asked me.

"Yeah sure, this is my application; anyone of you go ahead and have the work done. "

"No way, I am not going," Lingo told me, looking at Pastry.

"What about you?," I asked Pastry, who also shook his head.

"Ok I am going, but you both go and pay the advance money for the flat," I directed them and went to the administration block, carrying the three applications.

After some time, I called on Pastry's cell and the conversation went like this:

"Our applications have been rejected," I told Pastry.

"But why? We have already paid the advance money," Pastry screamed.

"It's because of the rule that we can't leave the hostel in between the running semester and that's why the administrator completely rejected the applications."

And the landlord refused to return our money back.

I felt like shouting a big Noooooooooooo... and just wanted to close my ears. I desperately needed peace of mind and a good environment to start afresh. And with that desperation, I moved my application to the senior-most person in the administration and somehow managed to quit the hostel.

I just took my luggage and moved straight to a nearby location. Wow!! What a beautiful place it was. Exactly what was required by me. The place was newly inhabited and so very few people lived there. The environment and the lack of rush attracted me like iron to a magnet.

So I welcomed my life in the new place, feeling full of confidence and freshness. It was a single room having attached services and well furnished, on the second floor of the building. It met my idea of independence completely.

And I started my studies with great excitement and for the first time got some books issued from the college library.

Meanwhile, Teddy, Genie and Khauf too were present there.

Khauf lived with his group of friends.

And Teddy with Genie, as they were like two sides of a coin.

And again, the days passed and we made memories out there hanging out at the tea stall near the toll plaza, gossiping, puffing and taking sips of tea.

One fine day, Khauf approached me for taking me as his flat-mate. Actually, he was having some financial problems and he desperately wanted someone to share his room. On the same day, Teddy too approached me for the same.

But the fact was that Teddy's flat was party-prone and if I had stayed there, I'd have to sacrifice my strength which I got from my peace of mind and being alone. Also, Teddy was able to pay for his expenditures.

I thought best of relations had gone sour after by staying together. So I decided not to stay with Teddy.

But I said yes to Khauf, in order not to lose my concentration and my peace of mind, which I had maintained from the previous two months or so after that black-night birthday party of Chaman and after getting our applications rejected by the administration.

I shifted in with Khauf and his other friends who

were less known to me.

And the three-bedroom flat looked good with a park in front. Khauf, the Gentleman and Mama were each having their separate rooms and girlfriends. The Gentleman and Khauf had personal issues so they had to be left alone without anybody's interference. I must tell you about Mama; he was born intelligent but was child-like sometimes and this childish behaviour irritated everybody in the flat.

Gentleman, who was straight forward, a quality that I liked in him the most, and introvert, was always ready to help.

But, the most significant change I observed was in Khauf's attitude. He was a completely changed man. Recalling that first day at cafeteria, I really found sea change in him. He was more willing to learn things now. He had become a tough guy like any other engineer.

After settling down, one fine morning when we were about to leave for college, one of our batch-mates, Danny, came, taking deep breaths and having some spots of blood on his shirt.

"What happened?," Khauf asked him while I was trying to understand the situation.

"Nothing, just something terrible happened this morning," Danny replied.

"Will you describe? What exactly happened?," Khauf again asked him with his eyes getting bigger.

"I came up this morning with my girlfriend. And while she was waiting for me outside on the road, some stupid neighbours thought something was wrong and they started inquiring. Although I tried to convince them, they started beating me and my other flat-mates. And then, I too gave them some hard punches. And in the whole drama cops came and took everyone to the local police station. I escaped the situation anyhow…."

Danny narrated the story to us with a nervous smile on his face.

"What about other guys? How are they?," I asked, feeling slightly curious.

"Yes, they are not alright In fact, some of them were even bleeding," Danny replied with tears in his eyes.

"It's ok dear; everything is going to be alright. Need not worry. Just forget whatever happened this morning," We all consoled Danny, patting his back for his 'bravery'.

Danny later managed to somehow get his other flat-mates out from the local police station and later managed to switch over to another flat in the same locality.

However, this left a bad taste for us. Looking for Danny and his friends, locals would threaten us with dire consequences if we dared to help Danny hide in our flat.

It was mere two weeks since the incidence happened, when the washerman, who worked at a nearby place, came to our main gate and said,

"A girl wants to come up and meet any one of you."

All of us started having a nervous breakdown.

I was excercising in my underwear. On hearing that a girl wanted to meet us I rushed to the wash-room to change but slipped and got hurt in my left knee.

Khauf and Mama were missing from action. It was finally Gentleman who showed some courage and went out to see her.

He had a formal talk with her and then told me that everything was ok and that I could come out of the washroom as the girl was gone.

Khauf too came out of his room and started enquiring about the whole drama.

"Nothing much, she was just asking for any good networking book for her coming interview. And I gave her my own book. That's it."

Gentleman cleared the smoke out of everything and we relaxed.

"Very nice. It's not even a week here and a girl comes asking for a book... shouldn't she have managed it from somewhere else. She must have known about whatever happened here," I said to the Gentleman annoyingly.

The next day we came to know that the same girl approached Khauf for her mobile phone recharge.

"Ohh only you have guts in all of us!! Girls approach only you," I told Khauf while Gentleman smiled.

"You know what, it's quite surprising to know that you don't have a girlfriend…Really, I am not joking," Khauf said with a big smile on his face and the answer to that question was unknown to me.

I too found it a bit strange that I did not have a girlfriend while all others had one. The closest relationship was that between Khauf and his girl.

It was a co-incidence anything that happened on the day revolved around a girl.

Late in the night around 10:30 while we were having dinner Khauf's cell phone rang. It was his uncle calling.

" Where are you?"

"*Pranam*! I am here only in my flat, having my dinner."

" Don't tell lies, I had been trying your number for for the past one hour. Where were you busy? Were you talking to your girlfriend or were you having something more important to deal with?"

It was a perfect question answer session between a guardian and a child.

Khauf made excuses, blaming it on the network. though he had just finished talking to his girlfriend.

And listening to his conversation with his uncle, we had a laughing riot and had to hold our stomachs so that we wouldn't vomit the things out.

And then all of a sudden, my cell phone rang unexpectedly.

It was my mother.

My parents are my only God and no one else. And I used to be or perhaps still am the most innocent boy in our family, especially when compared to my two notorious older siblings. Both of them used to conspire against me and provoke my parents to scold me which they never ever did. but it was all in the good spirit of brotherhood.

"How are you?," Mom asked

"*Pranam Maa*! I am fine, just finished my dinner… what about you?"

"Me too all fine. Please clear one doubt in my mind created by your brothers."

"What is that *Maa*?"

"Do you have any affair with any girl be it in college

or anywhere?"

"Absolutely not, and what are you talking *Maa*?"

"It's good then, feeling much better now...actually, your brothers suggested to me to find out if you were studying well and not involved with any girl...."

"It's ok, my brothers are just impossible...they start any time! And what about Papa, how is he?"

"He is all fine, but busy writing a devotional story for a movie team.

"I can sleep feeling good now. And you too do your work. Do well in your assignments and all that...good night."

"Ok *Maa*, take care...good night."

And this time, my flat-mates laughed at me.

***

The great train robbery

Before I start here about the memorable train journey, I would like to mention two of my good friends who really were true to me throughout my four years.

To me, Mini was like an integral part of my life…an any time, any place friend for me. Recalling that incident of somehow managing drinks for our godfathers and that too after midnight, I must say that was the rise of Mini as a star; a very good mathematician as well.

Genie, on the other hand, was a God-sent gift for me. The first time when I met him, it was like the meeting of the kings of the two powerhouses in this world. He was a diehard fan of Shahrukh Khan. Whenever I met him, I was reminded of the famous sound track from Bollywood 'Kkkkk… Kiran, I love you', and then the music, although, there was no Kiran in his life. He ragged our juniors by making them watch this movie the maximum number of times; a great man with never-ending mileage for hilarity. I named him so because he was true to me, was diplomatic at times in creating humour amongst us friends and supported me with his best throughout the ups and downs of my engineering life.

The reason that I have to mention them here is that they changed the course of my life forever. It was so nice to have friends like them. While Genie was any time available in any difficult situation, Mini always stood beside me when it came to having fun.

We were into the third year of engineering. We were having serious studies and were working hard for our individual assignments and group projects. The results for the fifth semester were out, and almost everyone had passed. But the guy who couldn't make it to the final year with us was Mini. Actually, it was his extreme illness and his very uncaring attitude towards himself that let him down.

Mini couldn't digest this and it was like the end of the world for him and as a result of which suffered a severe heart attack.

"Mini is hospitalized," Genie came with this very inhospitable news to me.

"What are you talking? why? how?" I asked him, taken totally by surprise.

"Yes, he is in the ICU right now."

We all rushed to the hospital without wasting any time. The doctors told us that he had recovered but was still unconscious.

It was the most relieving news that I had heard for a long time. By the evening, everybody from our batch reached the hospital, praying for his quick recovery.

By observing such a big crowd out there, one of the nurses asked somebody if Mini was a union leader. But it was his selfless, innocent nature and our love and affection that had brought so many people to see him. Everybody was praying for him the whole night and finally the next morning, we were told by the doctors that he was out of danger.

It's me and Teddy once again, with the unforgettable train journey. Actually, we both were returning from Khauf's native place after attending a marriage ceremony.

We were having only one bag in luggage. But our seats were not confirmed and so we had to manage with only an RAC berth. It was very uncomfortable 28-hour long journey. Added to this, the train had the notorious record for not reaching the destination on time ever.

Yet, the wheels were rolling at their maximum speed and we were trying to enjoy snacks and cold drinks with the outer glimpses of the nature's beauty. It was manageable, until one Punjabi family boarded the adjacent compartment. The family had a sweet-looking 20-something girl who looked just awesome.

It was not me exactly but, Teddy who got attracted to her. I was trying to keep myself busy with the latest health magazine. Teddy was more concerned about the girl, and again and again pushed me into looking at her. For me, it was just a mere time pass and during the journey I avoided making direct eye contact with her. Maybe I was just shy.

Teddy seemed like the happiest man on earth to see that girl. In the process of impressing her, he almost did the pole dance in our compartment.

"Teddy, what are you doing man? Can't you be seated properly?"

He said, "if you have a problem, let's exchange seats."

Actually, the girl was in my front view and at Teddy's back. And since I was a little involved in the process, I agreed for the seat exchange.

It then became more comfortable for both of us. Teddy could easily make friends with that beautiful girl and I could focus on my magazine.

All of a sudden, a loud clapping sound started coming from somewhere, within the train. It didn't sound like the clapping for appreciation. I managed to understand what exactly the sound was just in time.

It was a group of trans genders who were begging in the train. It was about to turn ugly for all of us present in the compartment. I wondered how we were going to handle the situation in front of the girl and other passengers in the adjacent compartment.

"Oye Teddy! just say suck and run."

"Have you gone mad dear? For what?"

I told him, "Just look back and say suck and run."

Actually, the problem was that these unwanted people were causing a lot of problem and embarrassment to the people, and Teddy and I were not in the position to make fun of them in front of the girl we were trying to impress. It was also a fact that neither Teddy nor I had any change or money to spare and get rid of them.

They came in our compartment and I started acting like a mentally retarded boy, giving a look at my fingers

Teddy took chance and started sending romantic songs to that device, without any hesitation.

"Ohh really...she has accepted my proposal. I can't believe this, yes, I have done it!," was Teddy's excited reply and he gave me a high flier.

For confirmation, we both looked at her and she was having a nervous smile on her face, any how, she clicked her right eye for Teddy.

Teddy was about to derail in the train and went crazy for her.

The journey had entered its last course though we wished it to go on forever. The worst part was that the stupid train was on time for the first time in its history.

We were just a couple of minutes away from reaching our destination and it was making us feel extremely sad.

"We are about to reach Teddy," I said.

"Not yet, one final touch is remaining," he replied, keeping me in suspense.

Teddy took out a piece of paper, wrote his phone number, his e-mail id and showed it to her with hope.

"I am keeping this piece of paper here on this vacant seat. Let's see what happens," he said confidently.

Saying this, he made a gesture to the girl and kept the piece of paper on the vacant berth as she had to continue her journey further.

Once we deboarded the train, we kept looking at the window. To our surprise, the girl too kept looking at us. She had picked up the piece of paper. A very pleasant and satisfying end to a great train journey, I thought.

On our way back to our rooms, Teddy received a

and moving my head up and down haphazardly. And that managed to rid me of those stupid people. They became more focused on Teddy and asked him for money. Consequently, Teddy had to pay them fifty rupees.

The girl opposite us was observing the whole drama and started laughing endlessly but in a stifled way.

Before Teddy could understand what was happening, I asked him, "Ohh...go have a chance, be a man, what are you doing? That girl laughed at you and you are looking at her as if nothing happened."

"Ohh yes... sure, I will," Teddy replied, getting a mental boost.

Teddy set about to finalize this whole drama. While observing that she had a handset in her hand, the idea clicked in his mind. He took his phone out and switching its Bluetooth on started searching for the devices in range. After failing for two consecutive times, Teddy started feeling a little frustrated.

I understood his problem and advised him I advised him to do it while having a close and direct eye contact with her.

"Ohh really," he replied, his eyes wide open in surprise.

Teddy gave his last try with a direct eye contact with the girl and, finally, his cell phone screen started displaying "still searching."

It was one of the most exciting moments for me too, as I watched the girl's hands moving on her cellphone. Teddy's cellphone was displaying the awaited information– "One device found in range, the Punjabis."

missed call from a strange phone number. He immediately called back. The receiver was none other than that beautiful girl and he continued talking to her till 4 am the next morning.

So, finally, Teddy was all set with his girl.

***

Back to campus

Our third year of engineering had one terrible module named DWDS, which dominated most of the semester. Our professor's demands on us combined with his never-ending lectures on database theory.

The announcement from the lecturer one morning left us feeling very sad. We had to develop an online solution for a business organization, which was a very large and intricate project. Both Teddy and I were good in designing a website but poor in coding the pages for a smooth functioning of the database.

"This module is very important Teddy, and this assignment carries almost 60 per cent of the total marks," I reminded him, with frustration writ large on my face.

"Ohh yes, sure, it's very difficult for me to learn and implement the things in this assignment. I don't think you can do that alone in such a short span of time," Teddy said.

"So what should we do? We have to complete this assignment somehow." I told him, thinking about my grades.

"Yes, you can approach Peter; he is a master in coding. He can do it. In fact, only he can do it. And you have good relations with him as well. So, go and ask him," I suggested.

"Ok, let me see," Teddy looked uncertain.

And so, for designing the complete pages of the proposed website for that business organization, Teddy went to Peter.

"Hi...what's up?" Teddy asked Peter.

"Nothing much, doing this assignment, You know that. Don't you?," Peter said, a little irritated.

"Yes I know that; you are a good laborious student. So, how much is done?"

As soon as Teddy asked this, Peter shot back, "You just go to hell, I don't have time. This is not an easy assignment. It requires a lot of hard work. Is that ok with you?"

This was a devastating for Teddy, not expected from a good friend.

"If I am going to hell, I will carry you with me...you are not worth the friendship. I approached you only when I completed the designing part. Anyway, I have to complete this assignment, and I am not coming to you again. You better do your work and in a better case just suck and run."

Thus, taking note of the situation, Teddy and I started working together on that bullshit assignment.

"Hey Teddy... our login page is ready, do click on this submit button," I asked Teddy. But the fact was that we had that much only and that too from the internet and books.

"Yeah it's good, but what about others? What about that tracking part?," Teddy inquired.

"Huh...does the tracking part involve finding the exact location of the goods which have been delivered to the customer from the organization?," .

"Yes...so, what should be the next step? I mean what should be the logic in the coding for that part?," He asked.

"Yeah, I have the solution. The first –it should be the complete headache of the organization to tell about the exact location of the goods to the customer. Alternate–we can have a dog or in a worst case, a good strong horse running parallel to the vehicle delivering goods to the customer. And these two would inform the customers whenever they want to know."

I thought that was enough, and asked Teddy for a confirmation. But we both started laughing, looking at each other.

Now, as the time for the submission of the assignment came near, we managed somehow to complete the system and started for the documentation for the same. We were really determined to get it done.

In the process of completing our documentation part, one earthquake-like situation erupted for Teddy. On the day of submission of the assignment in the lab, Teddy saw a couple and the boy was none other than Peter. It was like a volcano eruption for him."

At 5:45 in the evening on the same day, Teddy made a call to Peter saying, "If you have time, do come in the cafeteria as soon as possible."

Peter turned up, and Teddy said to him, "So, how was your submission dear? I hope it was a beautiful one! You know what Peter...you are not worthy of friendship. You are an asshole. You have time to help your girlfriend, that bitch. But, not for helping your friends...! Golu and I have submitted our assignments. But, it's a matter of time you showed us down. And even now, I can't believe you can be so cheap."

And then, a disaster occurred in their good friendship. Teddy slapped him and in return Peter punched him hard on his face. I had to intervene to stop them.

During Teddy's emotional speech, I observed that he was about to cry for his good friend who couldn't understand his feelings and refused to help him when he needed it badly. It was a bitter lesson for me as well.

***

Party time

All our internals, assignments and externals finally ended and we were waiting for our results feeling very relaxed. We had nothing left to do and were completely free. All we did was attend parties. We came to our fourth and final year, with the difficulty level increased to almost double the first year.

The FYP was the only concern in everyone's mind, so we were quite busy right from the beginning. From selecting a proper topic and making a draft proposal for our final-year project to the project manager, everything was hectic. My first draft proposal got rejected. But I again prepared it and the revised version was approved by the project manager. It was finally time for allotment of the supervisor and the advisor for the project.

Everyone was gossiping about their respective supervisors and the advisers. My supervisor was a strange man. While going to attend my first clinical meeting with him, I was busy thinking about his ifs and buts concerning my project. Anyway I walked up to his cabin and asked, "Sir may I come in?"

"Ohh yes, sure"

"Good morning sir."

He returned my greetings blandly. "Sir, I am developing one computer-based training application for the regular physical maintenance of the human body. And the project includes…," I started, after taking his permission to be seated.

I felt like the busiest boy on this planet while describing the special and core functionalities of my project.

"Ohh yes, your description sounds good. There is nothing to reject overall; do the best research work for your project. All the best," was his surprisingly gentle reply.

I thanked him and went out feeling relaxed and happy. I started working hard on the project to get the best outcome like everyone else. Apart from all this, one more important thing was going on in my mind. I was thinking about how people change, taking lessons from the Teddy-Peter fight. Why friends like Peter tend to become selfish and that too for a girlfriend. Peter had helped his girlfriend in almost every aspect in that assignment. How can a boy be so much loyal to his girlfriend but not to his male friends at the same time?

I do agree that helping others is good but doing it at the cost of good friends was something I couldn't digest.

I concluded that boys who have girlfriends are more brilliant than the ones who don't and have an edge over other ordinary students. But the fact remained that Peter and Teddy were true friends and Teddy deserved Peter's help in any case.

And at some stage of life, everybody needs someone special with whom life can be shared other than family members and friends to make life more beautiful.

So, why not give a try to support my theory?, the idea came in my blank mind.

I was a true supporter of the fact that every relation in this world should have the base as friendship, to make life easier, to have a better understanding of it and to make it less complex in many ways.

As all of us were busy in our projects putting in extra efforts, we had less time to share with each other. For me, it was like less fun in life and as a result I was not enjoying my life fully. Working on the project was a good thing, but it created differences among friends. Any of the songs which demonstrate a sense of loneliness would have supported what I felt.

So finally, I decided to go for a girl. Not for love or for making me a laborious student for my assignments but for true spirit of friendship.

In the process, I had the worst of experiences with bad girls, from many parts of the world compelling me to do wrong things. Searching inside the campus was like inviting an unnecessary conflict with my other male batch-mates. In fact, it was a strange kind of a situation. It was a situation like one to many and many to one relation. I didn't like it as it had all the makings of a family drama. I kept thinking what to do and the solution to it was beside me all the time–Internet.

It took me a while to have a girl friend but finally I

did manage to have one.

The girl's name was E.coli. "What the hell is this name after all?," I asked her.

"E.coli is the name of a bacterium, 'Escherichia coli' and I am a biology student," she replied gently.

"Ohh…I get it. E.coli, then "B.coli" must be one of your sisters or brothers," I joked, with a smile on my face.

She got angry and emotional.

"It's ok…it's ok. But, what is your real name and where are you from?," I asked her, as it was becoming necessary for me to know that.

"Oh yes… but, what's in the name? It's not necessary for me to tell you my name and I can tell you one thing that I am from Pakistan."

"Ohh really…!!" Frankly speaking, I was more than excited to have a friend from my first neighbouring country. And I was just as determined to make her my friend, as I was for my research. But, the only knowledge I had about Pakistan was that people from there moved to different parts of the world and conducted suicide attacks and other bomb blasts.

And I was having two options for my life ahead; either to hate or to love. In my case, a default condition was that I couldn't hate anybody. So, I continued climbing on the stepladder of friendship.

It was really exciting for me to know about how people in Pakistan reacted to Indians–normally or abnormally.

And I asked her an honest question. Her answer was as honest as my question. She said Indians were most favoured in Pakistan. We love Indians more than any other visitor. People get excited when they come to know that the person in front of them is from India."

For me, her reply was like a real nice feel-good factor.

But, I thought it was not the perfect reply. We have traditional conflicts. I asked her again.

"Yeah, sure, as far as war and cricket are concerned, people get crazy over here. But, the television dramas from India are so good. We love watching them. We really enjoy," she replied, as if she wanted to continue expressing her feelings endlessly. And then continued, "Look, I don't have any issues with you being an Indian."

"Yup, sure, I too don't have any problem with you being a Pakistani. It happens the same way here in India. We like to interact with people from your side, especially people like you."

In between the conversation, I was thinking that cricket was good, but war was a problem we developed for ourselves. For the first time, a very strange emotion was within me and it was killing me.

"Ohh…I am getting late now. Got to go. See you later. Bye!," she said, concluding the conversation.

"It's Ok. Take care," I said ending our first conversation.

With hardly a week spent talking with her, I came to know that the next Monday was her birthday. It filled me with excitement for the celebrations.

I wished her a very happy birthday and gave her my best for her career and life when the day finally came.

But, it was all happening through mails and chatting. The real feelings and emotions were missing in it , which I regretted.... But I really felt proud in helping her in anyway possible, it be supporting her with motivation or helping her in academics.

However, putting a lot of emotions can be very devastating. And as a result, I started having nightmares. Something special was happening to me strangely and it kept happening endlessly.

I tried my best to avoid those dreams but couldn't; even for the sake of my research work.

Cut, cut, cut!!!

I said to my life and moved to the balcony to check what exactly had happened to me. And what I found was that everything looked colourful and beautiful, with the colours all getting merged. The park in front was full of flowers and I really felt like love was in the air.

I was in the biggest dream of my life with someone special....

***

Winds of change

There was a time when I never cared for love and affection for a girl, at least not for the nightmares that caused so many unexpected twists in life. It was all like an ubiquitous computing module's presentation.

One day, I was to give my presentation on ubiquitous computing module as a group work demonstration.

"A very good morning to you sir, here I am with my presentation on the current status of the ubiquitous computing. So, to start with…."

I took out a balloon, and started inflating it, but it burst.

The lecturer said, "So, is this the only thing you have done in your project till now? Start working hard otherwise you will suffer. So, what is ubiquitous in your project?"

"Sir, I don't know, perhaps it's hidden," I replied nervously.

"To hell with your project!," he was furious.

"Sir, at least tell me how much can I score in this module?," I asked gently.

"Get the hell out of here, idiot," the lecturer roared

and I nearly went invisible only to realize that I was daydreaming, as the module was a real complex one with its diversities and implementation.

But, the same thing was happening to me everyday. I had fallen in love with this girl and was hardly devoting time to the research work I was supposed to be doing. All the time I was feeling something special.

It was a great feeling. I went ahead with the relationship without caring for the consequence. The first time I saw her I wished I could keep watching her face for the whole of my life sitting in my chair with a hot mug of coffee on the table. Actually, I should have been a poet to describe her beauty. I was really getting high on emotions.

Whenever I talked with her, I put my headphones on with the best of romantic songs playing to give some special romantic effect to the conversation. For the first time I started listening to *ghazals*.

I found myself completely swallowed with my feeling and wanted to do something special for her. One morning, I woke up with an idea that even if I were unable to visit her and express my emotions to her directly, I could do something else. So, I plucked a beautiful rose and took a snap of mine with the same and made a greeting card for her. I do not know from where I gathered that courage and mailed that snap to her.

She seemed overjoyed. Soon I received compliments from her. I thanked her for not deleting the rose. After this there was no looking back. Every moment I felt like sleeping so that I could see her in my dream.

In one of the dreams I felt like flying a fighter plane,

mistakenly in Pakistan and the Pakistani Army trying to stop me.

"Wait for an hour, I will be back, I have to see a girl…," I pleaded.

I became a complete fool thinking only about her.

My externals were about to start and the preparatory leave was on. On a pink cold romantic day, while chatting with her, she asked me, "What about your exams?"

"Ohh yeah, they are starting day after tomorrow."

"Are you sure?," she asked me.

"Yes… I am damn sure."

"Your exams are approaching and you are chatting with me…it's very bad."

"Not a big deal, I am all prepared."

She asked me about my academics, and did her level best to provide me the concepts of the module of my coming exam. That turned out to be a good experience for me. Somewhere I got my answer to the question bothering me.

A better understanding between friends can lead to success. But, it has to be selfless…without any hatred, without taking the other person for granted and last but not the least–not at the cost of anything.

In a very quick span of time, a lot of emotions got mixed up with my research work. Having emotions, feelings and sentiments were like so strange but special for me and that too for a girl; a new and beautiful experience. For me, it was not at all like she was from across the borders.

But, being an Indian I had to consider the emotions of those who were killed in any of the terrorist attacks. I had to know her opinion about terrorism, but I was afraid that the conversation would turn bitter.

This all started with her asking me about my dinner.

"Yes I have taken my dinner, had some non-veg."

"So, you like non-vegetarian food?," she asked.

"Yes sure… whatever we have, we take that as food. It's all about hunger…."

"So, what do you think about terrorism?," I asked.

"Yes, I can understand your feelings. Look, terrorism should not be the issue between us. It can never be defended. It feels really miserable to see what they have turned this beautiful life into. You never know what is going to happen the next moment, but you know it is all-pervasive. Have a look at the situation in Pakistan. You will hear suicide bombings and blasts happening every now and then. It is no doubt very frustrating.

"Heheh… and if you ask me anymore about terrorism, I am going to do a suicide attack on you," she said with an innocent smile.

"Ohh…ok ok."

"I was just kidding," she replied.

"Terrorism has become a world-wide issue now. Look, innocent people are being killed here and there. Do you know about Taliban?"

"Yes, Osama Bin Laden is there. So, the whole of this world knows about Taliban. I believe, Osama Bin Laden are two guys and if Osama without Laden proved so devastating, what would happen if they worked together."

"Hehehe," she smiled.

"No, it's not like that. Osama Bin Laden is a single person" she clarified.

"But, I hate the Talibans; they have ruined the spirit of our religion," she said.

"It's ok dear, whatever,... innocent people are being killed without any reason," I replied. I didn't want to push her directly or indirectly. "I have sympathy for the people who have been killed by these ugly terrorists. Now, suppose if these crazy people encourage India-Pakistan conflict and neither of the two nations exists, what would happen?," she asked unexpectedly, with angry emoticons visible on her face.

"Then, both of us will not be able to meet at least!"

"Heheh."

"What is this smile? Why don't you laugh with your heart open like hahahahahahhhh?" I asked her, feeling annoyed.

"It's ok dear, for you only... Hahahhah..." This time she was looking very good laughing.

"Anyway, tell me one thing. How much destruction will there be if one wants to use a nuclear bomb?" she asked.

"Ohh no...nuclear impact is very high. Dear...much more than we can imagine."

"Then India would require two-three bombs, and Pakistan some eight-nine to destruct this whole sub continent.

"Hahahahahahhhh," she laughed her heart out.

"How crazy are people, everybody knows nothing is

permanent, still they develop weapons. How crazy… we have our fresh water resources decreasing by the day in spite of both the countries possessing big water resources. Can't we instead of producing nuclear bombs develop technologies to convert this water into fresh drinkable water," she said, pouring her feelings out.

"Yeah sure why not, very well said madam….I really appreciate your ideas, your thinking, and you as well…," I said, getting attracted to her even more.

Gauging my state of mind, she said, "Absolutely not, we are just good friends… it's not like how you are thinking," she said, clearing up the matter. She rejected me before I could even propose to her.

"It's ok dear no problems…" I replied with fear in my eyes of losing her.

"Hahahhahhhhh… I am unable to understand, how could you even think of me as your lover? I mean, I am from Pakistan…don't you have any girls back in India?" She asked me this question with a bigger smile on her face. I blushed and found myself short of words to answer her.

"If you really want to know why I am attracted to you or your feelings, then you should know that you really have a good heart and beautiful thoughts. You speak your mind boldly. I mean, very few people are able to have such clarity of thoughts."

"But again, you are not supposed to fall in love with a Pakistani girl."

"According to the government census report, there are 940 girls to 1000 boys in India… and I believe I fall in the last 60."

“Hahahhhhhh… you are so funny”

“Agni…dear, it seems to me as if you are not at all a religious person,” she seemed curious to know.

"Why are you asking me this?"

“It’s like the way you live your life. I mean you eat non-vegetarian food, must also be smoking and drinking, and to top it all you are attracted to a girl different religion and nation,” she replied, using a combination of assumptions and facts.

“Look dear, as far as I am concerned, you can say that I am a non believer. I don’t believe in the existence of god or religion. And as far as my habits are concerned, yes I do drink and smoke and I love eating non-vegetarian food within certain limits. I basically appreciate the feeling of self belief, confidence and the passion for life. Only you can support and help yourself. And when you have the self belief you can win this world. People do talk about their faiths, luck, fortunes and all that… but I feel these are mere excuses for their life’s failures or achievements. Why don’t people understand that whatever is the outcome of their work, it’s totally the result of their working attitude….”

“But, what about those values and cultures through which this world survives? How many times do you go to a temple?”

“My dear, what values you are talking about? Those values out of which people make excuses to kill each other? I really wonder sometimes, why people are so insecured that they even move to the extent of killing each other.”

“Actually, I should say that, after the creation of this

beautiful world and evolution of mankind, people framed certain rules to follow. I don't have any problems with those rules but at the same time, the same rules are taking this world nowhere. Overall, religion created division among common people. It gave birth to hatred. *Hate him he is of that religion; kill him he is of that religion,* this is what you hear everywhere. So, it's better to lock the box of religion and be free with your thoughts and mind."

"And as far as the temple and prayers are concerned, I have been to nearly every place of religious importance and learned nothing, to be honest. For me, it's not like I offer prayers to god. I believe my parents who have brought into this world are my gods and I owe it to them."

"How strange!!"

"Look, I have some 'bad' habits like smoking and drinking, but as long as it is not hurting others it is fine."

"So, what according to you is crime?"

And again, while answering her questions, I never hesitated and continued with my thoughts, "For me, crime is to lie to someone, to kill innocents, and to do all that...I am sure you understand."

"What about your concentration? How do you concentrate to improve your performance?" Once again she had a question for me...

"Yes it's easy...whenever I am having some problem or need good concentration to work, I just talk to myself and at the next moment, I have the solution for the problem... and then I feel good to work with all that peace of mind."

"All your descriptions sound interesting and impressive to me."

"Look, if there is God, it's ok. I mean I don't have any problem. I know people can have a different opinion from me and you already have one."

"But, even then I would insist that you should go to temples and pray to God and you must quit smoking and drinking right from this moment if you ever want to talk to me again!" she retorted unexpectedly.

"Ok dear, I will try. You know, I don't want myself to be bound by anything, I am a free person; I just want to be independent. I am fine without God. I really find this entire concept very boring and unexciting. Religion for me means festivals, and yes, they are fun. At least, they provide moments of happiness and reason to celebrate," I said, trying again to explain to her my overall concept of religion and God.

"Ok now, I am feeling sleepy. So, good night… take care," she said, wrapping up the conversation. "Yeah sure, sweet dreams and good night," I wished her back, liking her caring attitude towards me.

Every morning I started reading newspapers and particularly looked for news about Pakistan. The worst part was that almost every day, there was news of bomb blasts and suicide attacks from across the border, which always made me worry about her. She had become so precious to me…

Anyway, one fine night, it was all foggy and I was waiting for her to be online, covering myself in blankets and sending offline waiting emoticons and some messages like: *where are you? Where the hell are you? Are you dead somewhere? Where exactly are you? What happened? Are you alright? Is there something wrong?*

She finally came online around 1:30 in the morning.

"Where were you?"

"Ohh, so sorry dear I am late today..."

It turned out that she had gone for a movie with her hostel friends.

Suddenly she said, "Ok, I am tired now, going to bed. Good night, sweet dreams and take lots of care of yourself..."

I was really disappointed by the way she talked to me that night and decided to check if she really had emotions for me.

The whole night I could not sleep. Early morning, I sent her an offline message:

My results are out, I have failed in one of my modules... and that's why, I am going to commit suicide...

And by afternoon, as I was on my sms status, I received a reply from her: *You are not going to do anything to you. You will get another chance. So better start preparing for that...and I will help you in doing that.*

Are you getting my messages? Why are you not replying to me? Are you dead already?

Hello...you there? This was accompanied by sad and angry emoticons together.

And then, I finally got the answer and it was quite satisfying for me to know that, she really cared for me...

Anyway, I went online and clarified that it was all fake.

I explained it was all to be sure of her care.

"Damn you, Agniwesh, I was about to call you… how could you do this to me?" She said showing ultimate angry emoticons…which made her look even more beautiful.

"I was just kidding… I am so sorry," I apologized.

"Don't you dare, talk to me again… how stupid you are…" she said, with angry and 'not talking to you' emoticons.

"Ohh no, please… don't say that. I have good grades overall. I can't even think of failing again."

"Go to hell…" was the final reply from her.

I regretted what I did to her and said sorry every day for more than a week, every time finding her offline.

I finally found a cute reply from her like, "It's ok… sorry granted."

The days passed and we talked for hours.

To me, her friendship was an indelible print left on my life from someone very special; a gift for me from life. But, the worst thing was that she refused to give me her cellphone number, saying she didn't want to talk to me whole night like lovers.

But, at the same time she was having my cellphone number saved as "Agent butterfly" in honour of my compliments to her. Whenever I admired her about her looks and thoughts, she would call me a butterfly for ever buttering.

One fine night again, it was getting dark and winds of love were blowing…and suddenly, she wanted to see the place where I was living. Although we were using our laptop camera for video chat, she wanted me to give her the sight of the place.

The best option for us was using the Google Earth.

"Do you have the Google Earth in your laptop?," I asked her.

"Yes, I have. But needs to be installed."

"How much time does it take to get installed?" She asked, looking impatient.

"Not much."

Our conversation resumed after a few minutes taken for the installation.

"Yup, it's on now… what will I have to search for?"

"Ok, type in the search bar of the application Sec-18." "And what I will have to search?" I asked in return, feeling excited.

"Type BIO UNIVERSITY, Islamabad"

"Good…ok. Did you find anything?," I asked curiously.

"Yeah, I can see a big-big ground. So, do you guys play football or *kabaddi* out there hahahahhahahahhhhh….?"

"No, it's not like that. It's a newly inhabited locality and I roam around here in the parks and on the roads where I feel free, with you…Hahahhah," I replied, with a little smile of my own.

"With me, how come dear?"

"Yes with you only…like the music I have on my I pod, your memories," I replied, trying to sound romantic.
"How romantic… Great, I like that…" she replied curtly as expected, as she didn't want to be in love with me.

Even after several attempts, she wasn't able to exactly locate my house.

"Ok, leave it..." I said finally, feeling dejected.

"What about BIO UNIVERSITY? Did you find that?," she asked with excitement.

"No, the installation is still going on."

"What installation?" she asked doubtfully.

"Dear Ms E.coli, the installation process of Google Earth is still going on in my laptop. And I really don't know why it is happening so slowly. Actually, I don't have the setup."

"Damn you Agniwesh... I am not talking to you," she wrote, getting angry and showing some angry emoticons.

"It's ok. Next time I will search BIO UNIVERSITY for sure"

"Very good, I appreciate that."

"Ok, now if I come to your window looking straight at you... what will you do then?" She asked unexpectedly.

"Ohh, is that so? Then I would hold you tightly and would never allow you to go back," I replied, clearly expressing my feelings.

"How romantic... but you know what I will do? Call your landlord. And then he will throw you out of his house," she replied with the kissing emoticons.

"Then I will take you to one lonely place, where only we would be there and nobody else to disturb us," I replied, sending kissing emoticons to her.

And amazingly, she just showed me the blushing emoticons and ran out of words. .

"Ok, I am going to bed now...sweet dreams, good night."

"Hello madam, what happened? Are you alright?" I asked to confirm whether she had any problems with me.

"No, nothing happened... just feeling sleepy. Ok, sweet dreams and take care."

"Ok then. Have a good night. Sleep well..."

Over the days she asked me to send her some songs, whose download websites were blocked and so I ended up sending her many-many songs.

I didn't even realize that this was the best time of my life. The date-sheet for my final-year project presentation arrived. It was high time I geared up for the same. On the night prior to the presentation, I re-read my documentation of about 170 pages, checked the application developed for its functionalities to see if it was working properly and finally made some PowerPoint slides to better demonstrate my work." The next morning, I woke up early as usual and the first thing I did was finish a car racing game that I had found very difficult to complete. So, after getting a good, positive and confident start to the day, I took a bath and took my parents' blessings on the phone.

Now, the time was nearing to make history and I was about to exit my house to go for the presentation, specially dressed for the occasion when suddenly, my cellphone rang with a number starting from +92-! I could not believe it. It was like daydreaming.

Anyway, with some nervousness and excitement I took that call. It was E.coli. It took me a while to get over her the fact that I was talking to her. She wished me all the best for my presentation.

It was really nice of her to be so caring for me. All the way to the college I kept thinking of her sweet voice. As I reached my college, my friends complimented me that I looked very happy and good. It was E.coli effect, I thought.

I reached the presentation hall and stood like the sword of the great Sir William Wallace before my supervisor and the adviser.

The day proved to be the most happening day of my life. I answered every question asked by the supervisor and the adviser confidently. Not to mention that I received my first international call from someone I really loved. Her call made me desperately want her for my life.

I was becoming an engineer, but I felt like a child who just got the most precious gift of his life. Her sweet voice kept echoing through the day. The distance between us was killing me; in fact, I was dying to see her.

And in the night, she was online again. And I decided to take one more chance, for the sake of my useless research work which turned out to be my love in true sense actually!!

"Hi," I said, feeling love struck.

Buzz!! And again a buzz, was her reply.

"What happened?"

"What would happen to me!! I am all fine and I just wanted to give you a call one more time, to ask you about how you fared in your presentation?"

Ok, I am done with my engineering now, I am now a "bachelor"... of engineering and I did excellent in my presentation today, all credit goes to you. I answered every questions my supervisor and adviser asked me. And I really appreciate the way you treat me. Is this not enough reason to fall in love with you? I replied to her with all my excitement.

"Ok, that is good and don't think of yourself very smart.... Just delete my contact number from your phone book," she ordered me showing ultimate anger.

"Anyway, I have some plans for you this night. Will you give me some time for that to execute?" I asked.

"Yes I will...and why not! You are very good to me."

By that time, I had some idea about her personal life. But I didn't inquire about it so not to ruin the spirit of my planning for her.

"It's ok dear, not an issue...will take your problems one by one and try to solve them."

"Ok tell me one thing do you enjoy looking for things which are beyond scope?"

"Not so... I mean I didn't get you. What is that "beyond scope" and how to do that?"

"Need not to be so sad... I am here. I will do that for you."

"I have a plan for you this night and I need your mind concentrated in Sydney."

"What? What concentration of mind? I mean what exactly you are going to do with me in Sydney?"

"Ohh...don't be scared. I am here and I will be there with you as well. For me, I need not concentrate; that's why I told you to concentrate and after that we will move to Sydney tonight only. All you need to do is to start imagining that we are in Sydney, Australia."

"Ohhh...wow!! That is great. I mean, give me some time and I will be back... no, tell me what exactly I should have; I mean what I should wear this night with you for the opera house? she asked.

"You can have a white or farm green frock and your hair open," I replied imagining her beauty in the clothes I suggested.

"Ok ...I will be back, Just wait for me."

"Ok dear I am here. Take your time."

When she returned, I was stunned. She really was wearing the same clothes in complete green "with white spots" frock.

"You are looking so beautiful in this frock."

"Thank you so much dear; and you too go and change your dress or you want to move to Sydney in the T-shirt and nicker you are wearing only..? I think you can have a neck tie on your presentation suit."

"Ok ...let me try. And, after some time, the journey to Sydney opera house started and I was with a girl looking awesomely beautiful on the streets of Sydney.

"Now what we have to do?" she asked me with a cute smile on her face.

"Yes, we are moving to the opera house! It's 11 in the night," I almost shouted in excitement.

"Yes I know that we are marching on the streets to the opera, but what is the need to be so loud so close to my ears; I am not dumb. Go to hell... and to hell with your opera."

"And you know what; you are looking more beautiful with this killing anger."

"And if you are going to utter another word, I'll give you my this…on your head," she replied, pointing towards her shoes.

"Ohh…ok I'll keep telling you that you are looking stunningly beautiful every time. Ok you do whatever you want to. Kill me, shoot me, hit me with your shoes or if possible drown me in this harbor."

"No, just shut up Agni…never ever utter those ugly words of death again; never in a joke even," and she held my hands.

"What to do now, the time is over for the opera," she asked, having a look at her watch.

"My dear, would you mind if I ask you out for a night walk?"

"Yeah sure…."

So, we both went for a long night walk as we missed the opera.

"So, you finished your engineering now; what are your further plans?"

"I don't have any plans right now"

"Ok…that's good, just now you have finished…I can understand. But, what about a job?"

"Job is not an issue for me. I can get a job any time… it's all about my choice."

"I would like to suggest you dear…don't take your life so easy…. Life comes to us randomly, we can have happiness and sorrows in a quick span of time… we even don't get to know about all that. So better plan for your future, take your time and start planning."

"Yes I understand all that… but, I need some time.

Right now I am with you and I don't have to do any planning for now at least. I'll manage all that…later."

"Ok, it's so good… at least you listen to my words. "Yes…I like to listen to you not because of your maturity… but, because of the fact that I like listening to your sweet voice. As simple as that."

Meanwhile, we reached the Sydney harbor and holding each other's hands for the first time…. I was feeling some kind of real love for her, as a result of which I proposed for a couple dance…and again she replied me the same way and I was almost killed by her beauty.

During those slow movements, I palmed her back and then on her waist…tightly, and then pulled her nearer to me, feeling the exact respiratory noises with her heartbeats on a high and having a direct eye contact… and again while doing that, I was about to give her my first kiss….

"No…no…leave me. I am sorry…," she said nervously with tears in her eyes, looking away.

"It's ok…I am sorry," I said.

"It's ok dear, need not say sorry…. I have certain restrictions and I can't go beyond them. Ok, let's move now back to our rooms.

I could not control myself and grabbed her right hand.

And again, making a direct eye contact, I proposed to her on my knees…

"I love you and you only, my every breath, my every heartbeat…my every moment is for you…I am here in this world so that I could love you and you only…you are all mine. And if you ask your heart…you will get my feelings… will you marry me?"

I was dying to hear those three words from her, "Yes I will..."

"Dear Agni... I wish I could be your lover. But...but, our religions won't permit that to happen. I mean, social barriers are there which won't allow us to be together forever," she replied, showing sad emoticons.

"It's ok...fine. No problems," I typed, without any emoticons. It was like the breaking of the longest dream of my life and tsunami of tears rolled down my cheeks.

And to be honest I felt like I was on the deck of the great and the beautiful Titanic asking for some space from Jack and Rose saying that your time is over now...

Life moved on. What I felt for her was not mere attraction; It was true love. The love, the affection, loads of chocolates and her amazing birthday gifts I can never forget. She was truly a gift from life.

Like there are always two sides to a coin, this story too had its flip side. I could never convince her for my love. To hell with her reasons.

And later on, when she was about to get engaged, we both by mutual consent decided to part ways, as even I didn't want to disturb her with my feelings anymore.

Though there was no filmi-ending to my love story, I continued to be her email friend. Albert Einstein was right when he said gravitation was not responsible for people falling in love. But, positive thoughts, good understanding and adopting the best way of living your life are sufficient to take you to the world of love. That's what I learnt.

***

Over to recession

Only the last two months were left of those golden four years. Though these two months were relatively relaxed there was no relaxation ahead, as we all had received our last installment from our parents and now they expected results. No good companies were approaching us, and the companies that did were taking full advantage of the great slowdown in the market.

What can one do with a salary of Rs 5000 per month? And that too with a bond amount ten times the salary. The salary wasn't even enough to buy food properly. So, the big question posed to us by life caused frustration in many of my batchmates, while others managed to keep their cool.

One day, Teddy and I were discussing our prospects with some friends, when suddenly I got a call from an unknown number. I received it to hear a familiar voice, "Hey Golu, what's up?"

It was one of my friends from back home, and it was good to know that he had survived the stupid recession.

"Hi Manja. I am fine. Just passing time, nothing

much. What about you?"

"Yeah, I am fine too. What about placements?," he asked.

"Ohh...yes, you first tell me about your college."

"It's good over here. Guys are being placed with good packages. Giant IT firms have approached our college. Overall, for us it has been good," he said jokingly.

"Here too, we have some good corporate houses approaching us. In fact, they have promised to take our whole batch, with best of packages. I even managed to get to the HR round but couldn't make it to the final. Let's see what happens next," I gave Manja a strong reply, to keep the momentum from my side although there were no placements happening, neither here nor there.

"So, what did they ask you in the HR round?," he asked, sounding excited.

"Yes, they asked me some basic C programming concepts…could manage only two out of the three questions. Dear friend, take my suggestion and stop studying Java, for the sake of your selection at least. Even I don't read Java anymore. It's a complete wastage of time."

"Ohh no…I wish I could be in your college. I am sure I would have had better chances of getting a good job," he said, disconnecting the call.

My friends were all laughing and Teddy said, "You are a scoundrel and nothing more than that with a big smile on his face."

"It's ok Teddy dear. You need to be on the upper side always. Look, I have an idea for making money and all

I need is some more friends who can work well together like a corporate, buddy."

"So, what are you going to do next?" Teddy asked me in surprise.

"Ohh yes, sure...let's move to other colleges, ask for some good money in return for placing their students in our fake company."

"What next?" Excitement was mounting.

"We will take only half the money, and distribute the remaining half to the finally selected candidates. We will continue operating until we get sufficient money, and after that we'll declare bankruptcy."

"What an idea, it's great," Teddy replied.

Recalling those slow, hot and humid days of summer during the recession, I have to say for the first time we checked cost of the food before ordering.

***

The re-union

During my engineering life, Genie had supported me tremendously. He was the one who gave me an identity among others, including the seniors. He was just great to me. However, there was to be one bitter side to our relationship as well.

During my friendship with E.coli, I never told my friends about her. I didn't want to unless something really good happened between us. All my friends found a huge change in me. Though I used to be physically with them, I did not belong there. Slowly, my friends too became indifferent to me.

This changed behavior of mine upset Genie the most. He genuinely was worried about me and sneaked into my profile account. Soon the whole circle of friends came to know about E.coli who I had kept under wrap for so long. For me, it felt like a betrayal. One night I was just checking my Facebook to know what exactly was going on, and saw Genie using the application, 'Know truth about the people around you' and his wall post revealed my story:

What does Agniwesh think about himself?

Many of our friends commented, *Agniwesh thinks of*

himself as Shahrukh Khan.

"I don't like this," I too wrote on the wall, which was full of comments from my friends, seniors and juniors. I felt terribly betrayed. I didn't waste any more time in calling Genie.

"Where are you dear?" I asked him, trying to hide my feelings.

"I am on the way back from Shimla. I am with the Holy man, will take around about three hours to be there with you" .

"It's ok…I will see you tomorrow." I didn't get any sleep all night.

Next morning, I went straight to him, and asked angrily,

"Why did you do this to me?"

"Ohh, look Golu, I am sorry for if my act has hurt you. I did not intend to hurt you. I am sorry once again."

"Your sorry is ok, but what about the hurt you caused?"

"Look, all this I did to find my best friend, who was lost somewhere. Life was so boring for me without you, and it was too strange for all of us to miss you," Genie said, with tears in his eyes.

And that was enough to melt my heart and mind. At that moment I realized the importance of good friends in life.

"And, what about your love life now?"

"It's over, she left me," I replied.

"Look friend, I am damn serious about the way you

are carrying on with your life...actually your love. You have been great to each one of us. But, you have become so dull...have a look at your face. You are not at your best. You have ruined your life and each one of us in the process. What makes you so unhappy? You know you are unhappy for something which never happened...listen, I can say by looking at your face that you are bemoaning your break up...but that is so foolish...you are feeling bad about a break up when the make-up never happened... just look how dull you have become...you stupid."

"You are a big rascal...bigger than I am," I hugged him.

Genie opened my eyes and put confidence back in me. He made me realize my foolishness and gave me the answer to the question for which I did that research. It was Peter's truly unprofessional and unethical attitude that had led to the rift between them. Peter's time management was poor, he should have helped Teddy. If he could help his girlfriend, he could have helped Teddy as well. I also managed to patch up with my friends. Softy felt happy.

The time finally came to bid farewell. We all had completed our final exams and graduated with flying colours. College life was in its last leg and a grand party was the best way to wind it up. It was Pastry, Lingo, Teddy, Jackie, Kapala, Saambha, Lucy, the Holy man, Genie, Mini, Oops and Peter who made the arrangements, using shoulder collections in which everybody contributed. We managed to collect some 80,000 rupees, which was a good money for a grand party.

We bought the best of vodka, champagne and salads

for our farewell. We also arranged Crazy lights and a DJ. We made some emotional farewell speeches. We all drank and danced whole night.

***

Love forever

The next morning, I woke up early as usual. It was a perfect day to get a hangover. The hangover of our lifetime. It was the last time we had the water splashes, drinking, dancing and pushing and pulling. Everyone was still unconscious sleeping where they had found space in the night, with legs and bodies entangling. And I was sitting with the newspaper and a glass of fruit juice, reading the same old news–bomb blasts, robbery, minister's statement on terrorism and all that.

On page two, there was news of a Pakistani couple who had come to New Delhi for their wards' complex operation, and had been successful. After reading the newspaper, I just looked at my cellphone and was quite surprised to see that there were as many as seven missed calls from E.coli.

My cellphone rang again. This time I received her call, said hi and inquired about her wellbeing.

"Will you please be online?," she asked. I immediately went online.

"How are you dear?," she asked me.

"I am all fine…we had a superb party last night. And I am having a deep hangover."

"You had a party! How many pegs did you have? Puffed enough cigarettes. Correct me if I am wrong."

"Ohh...so sorry dear, ok I promise this was my last. So sorry I broke my promise." I answered, though my eyelids still wanted to remain shut.

"I was just remembering my online trip to Sydney with E.coli!! That was so superb; I really enjoyed in your company that night. Really, you are so funny and a little bit naughty as well in your imaginations. I must say thanks to you for that night."

"It's all ok. But what is the need of that thanks? It was not only an imagination; it was actually my love for you, which led me to think like that and that too in your company," I replied with some irritation.

"Ok…it's all fine. So what did you do the whole time after we got separated?"

"My dear, I missed you so much. To be true I miss you 18 hours a day and during the next six when I am asleep, you come in my dreams…so I missed you every day and night."

"Where is Agniwesh?" she asked, showing crying emoticons.

"I am here only…"

"No, I am not talking about you…where is my Agniwesh?"

I was a bit surprised…

"No, I am here…right now; you are talking to Agniwesh only," I tried to convince her with my eyes wide open trying to confirm whether she had gone mad.

"No, you are not Agniwesh. He always lives in his hangover. He doesn't care about me anymore. He put me in to so much love and is now evading me. Where is he?" she asked me, showing crying emoticons again and again.

"What exactly has happened to you dear? Why are you crying?"

"No, nothing happened..."

But, again she showed me crying emoticons.

"It seems something wrong has happened to you."

"Baby happened,"

"Love happened"

"Wow, congratulations...!! Very good. All the best," I said, feeling emotionally low.

"You will never understand...my feelings. You are a big idiot"

"These songs are killing me and I can't live without you. I am in love with you and I want to be with you forever. We will settle down in Shimla...and I will take care of your needs...we will have a small house and in that we will have a mud house and...and...and we will live happily forever...so, either you come here, or I will be there for you only," she said and started showing lots of kissing and love struck emoticons, but she was still having tears in her eyes clearly visible on the web camera.

And to be honest I again felt like I was on the deck of the great and the beautiful titanic asking for some space from Jack and Rose and saying that your time is over now...

I decided to call her through yahoo call services...

"You know what dear, these tears and sadness does not suit your cute face...some days back, while having my lunch in a restaurant here, I saw a girl in the veil. And as she finished her lunch, she was moving to the wash basin with her face uncovered..."

"Then what happened?"

"Then what, she moved away from the restaurant with her family..."

"Just stop kidding...I said stop kidding to me!"

"Ohh so sorry dear...but, the best part about that girl was that she was looking like you and for a while I was trying to find you in her as she was moving to the wash basin...and in the process of all that neither of us realized that we were staring at each other and then out of shyness her face turned red and she covered her face again within no time"

And then finally, I realized that my single action could lead to multiple reactions over me from her family members and then a possible riot...

Hehe...a very low smile she gave while trying to wipe her tears on her cheeks. And I felt good as her tears stopped at last.

"And you know what Agni, you have not changed at all..."

"Yes you are right...I am against any of the negative changes in human thinking...and my thinking still loves to love you again and again...forever"

"You must know this as well…you would not be able to change my feelings for you, I love you and I have realized that I was wrong in not falling in love with you earlier. So, I have decided that we will settle down in Shimla and when you are coming here to take me in your arms full of imaginations which are the best thing to happen in my life all due to you only, and don't you dare to look for any girl whether she is having her face covered or uncovered," she said and continued ahead with her so many words…as if she didn't want to stop this time. But, she was deep in her emotions and feelings with tears in her eyes…which I found difficult to resist from my side.

And this was the time when my heart almost stopped working…I mean, I never expected this to happen in my life as far as she was concerned.

"Dear, I have the best of my feelings for you…I respect you and your feelings. You have been great to me and special for me for the whole of my life…but, at the same time, whatever you are saying is not possible…for now. I will welcome you here in case you are coming with my heart open for you, I will wait for you." I told her, showing nothing because I knew somewhere that she wouldn't come as it would be hard for her to sacrifice her family, her society and above all her religious commitments.

"Why is that so… Agniwesh?" she asked me.

"Because…because….I don't have any reasons, you should have told me this earlier, I am just unable to come and see you even. I mean, I don't have the first salary with me; and without that, I will ruin your life only," I tried to convince her with the feelings as if I had engulfed the whole of the whiskey bottle without mixing anything in it. That was really bitter for me to explain to her. But, any how I managed to continue ahead resisting my emotions for her...

"You go ahead and work for the betterment of your country and I will do the same here..."

"I want to send you a gift," I said, "A Pakistani couple is here in Delhi. And I want to send you a beautiful gift through them...for our friendship." I requested her showing hug emoticons.

"No, I don't want anything from you...to hell with the country, to hell with this world and you too just go to hell and I hate you...I hate you and I hate you only...," and she went offline.

At that moment. all I wanted was to stop that rectangular block mentioning "E.coli is off line" on to the right most corner of my laptop from sliding down forever...

The worst part was that, she was about to get engaged in the coming days and then about to get married...overall, I could not manage to bring her to India.

The whole of the assignments and academic tortures during engineering made me so strong as a human being, I could not even manage to cry aloud for her...but wanted to so much.

Exactly, this was the time for me to face the truth...a bitter reality for my life...and she was my love forever...

all I could manage to do was punch hard on the table saying damn it…in anguish and grief for her…

After that, all my friends, woke up from the hangover and went to their respective destinations….while I was still in the hangover of that true love which was really unconditional without any promises.

***